DIE and STAY HIDDEN

A NOVEL

Michael S. Bromberg

THE HAMPTON STREET PRESS
SAG HARBOR, NEW YORK

ONE

The water was cold. Too cold. It wasn't a good day for sailing. It was a worse day for swimming. John Street knew Dick would hate himself for having gone out on a day like this. As he swam, John wondered how long it would take Dick to come back on deck and realize John was gone. It was a small boat. So, once Dick got topside, there weren't too many places John could be. He had to be over the side.

John's sneakers were heavy. He wondered if he should take them off. He debated it as he swam toward shore. Would he be more conspicuous without shoes? Should he take them off and carry them? What if he lost one? What would he do then? What if it floated away? Had he ever heard of a case where they could tell from the shoes if they'd been taken off or dragged off the body? He thought, Surely, if the laces were untied and if they found the body—wait a minute, there isn't supposed to be a body!

As he swam, he worried that, being thirty-nine, out of shape, and not a good swimmer, he wasn't going to make it to shore. He should have thought of that before. He was struggling to stay afloat. As he tried to keep the water out of his mouth, he wished he'd made good on his resolution to take off the 15 extra pounds from his 6'1" frame and get into better shape.

Looking through the fog toward shore, he was trying to see a place to come out of the water, when he heard Dick calling. At first, he just called, "John?" But then it was the "Oh Christ!'s" and the sound of Dick's voice going into a higher pitch that told him that Dick was panicking because he couldn't find John on board. He tried to make less noise and swam. He liked Dick and was sorry that it had worked out this way. He thought to call out. To tell Dick he just fell over the side—but he swam on. This was the way it was going to be. He was committed.

John had never swum anything like the distance he had just traveled. He still had a way to go. He pondered if the presumption of death would be stronger if the boat were further from shore than a man like him could easily swim.

Through a small break in the fog, he saw the rocks of the channel wall up ahead. He looked back. He couldn't see the boat nor hear Dick. He knew he was still hidden from view. Then, he looked to see if anyone was around who would see him climb out of the water. No one.

It was all he could do to reach out his cold right hand and secure his hold on one of the rocks. He wrapped an arm around another rock and waited for the strength to pull himself up. He felt that he would never catch his breath. With his rubbery arms, he hauled himself up to where he could rest his chest on the rocks. He waited for more strength and then pulled himself up the rest of the way.

His heart felt like it would never stop racing. He wanted to go to his car and get the money. His fatigue made him wait. Fatigue then merged with the feeling that this was not really happening. He didn't know, if he closed his eyes, if he would fall asleep or if he was really asleep already.

He sat there in the Saturday morning fog and felt terrible about Dick out on the boat. He told himself he had just let himself go over the side rather than deciding to go. He told himself that if he had thought about jumping, and leaving Dick like that, he couldn't have. But after Dick went below to get the fog horn, the impulse to let the water dissolve his problems took control. He was over the side before he had a chance to reconsider.

Now, sitting on the rocks, in the thick fog, with his heart still pounding, he tried to gather strength and to concentrate, to see if he wanted to re-think his non-choice.

The night before, it was the smoke in the bar that had been thick. And the music much too loud. John sat in a corner booth and impatiently looked at his watch. He could hardly take his eyes off the women with their pimps.

John hated working on Friday nights. He told himself even though the money had been slow these past few months, he was too well established to have to work when he didn't want to. But he assured himself, this was a special situation.

He had the debate with himself as he waited: He thought, Hey, for this kind of money you can blow a Friday night.

No way! If the client wants you to represent him, make him come to you. The money should be no big thing. You don't sit in a joint like this on Hollywood Blvd. You don't chase money at the cost of pride.

He had had the internal debate about how far you should go to get paid before. But this time he was waiting for $150,000 in cash—as much as he had netted last year. So, he found himself in the bar with the pimps and their ladies waiting for a man who was already 30 minutes late.

A stunning redhead in a gold lamé micro mini walked by him on what looked like four-inch heels. Unlike the other women there, her makeup was not overdone. The dress came to just about the level of her wrists as she walked. She had a great figure with her white breasts bulging at the top and straps of the neckline. John envisioned her coming over and kneeling in front of him—doing things that his wife, Marsha, stopped doing right after they were married.

As she walked through the smoke of the bar, the girl watched John watching her. The way she made her living was, at least in part, based on knowing what men thought. In his three-piece suit with no tie, John, with his blue eyes and short brown hair looked like the tired lawyer he was. He couldn't take his eyes off her. He knew she was watching him on her way to the streets. He did nothing to alter her course.

He thought, I think I should pass around some cards here. Some of these bastards are going to need me soon. He shook his head, the girl noticed the movement and turned to see if it was a call to her. It wasn't.

What he was thinking of was "the crime cycle." She would go out and sell her services and give the money to the pimp. The pimp would get busted and give the money to John. Or she would get busted and the pimp would give the money to John to get her out so she could screw more guys called "Johns." He thought, All we need now is for me to pay this young thing for the pleasure of her services and the cycle will be complete.

His thoughts where interrupted when he saw Snappy enter the bar. Snappy was a big man and the long camel colored coat that was his trade mark made him seem much larger. No one could remember seeing him in public without that coat, a dark shirt, and black tie. Snappy saw John and started to turn his head away but he kept his eyes on John until John nodded. Then Snappy completed his turn and started making his rounds. He visited with someone at the bar, then a group of people off at a table.

John watched him, looked around at the scene, and thought about the fee. He watched Snappy turn from his talk at the one table and sit at another table. John looked at his watch and wondered how little sleep he would get before going sailing with Dick Moran in the morning. He watched Snappy, and thought of Dick.

John and Dick had both started in the District Attorney's office together fourteen years before. He thought, Dick stayed with the office, and I'm sitting here watching my hookers go out and earn my fee, while I wait to score a huge fee from a big-time smack wholesaler. Not bad. He shook his head.

He wasn't sure just how long he should wait for Snappy to make some kind of move. He was sure Snappy wasn't going to come and sit with him. When Snappy had called that afternoon, he just said that he wanted John to handle his case but didn't want to "put his business on the street just yet." John figured there was only one way to move the playacting along. He got up from his seat. When he saw that Snappy noticed, he put some money for his beer on the table and headed for the door. Snappy whispered something to one of the women at the table, waited until John was out of the bar, and then followed him.

John walked down to the corner and watched. When he could see that Snappy was out of the bar and saw him, John walked around the corner to the doorway of an appliance store. He stepped in.

When Snappy got there, John said, "Step into my office."

Snappy looked up and down the block, then frisked John with his eyes, and then stepped in. John had to suppress a smile. He thought, This guy has just come out of a bar full of thugs, pimps and hookers, he's the meanest son of a bitch in this or any other galaxy and he checks me out to see if it's safe to go into a doorway with his new lawyer! God damn that's class!

Snappy looked John in the eye. "My man downtown say they's comin' to cuff me on Monday. I gotta know that this case is gonna be OK." It was more like a question.

"Snappy, I'm not going to bullshit you. This one is not going to be easy. I'm only a lawyer not a magician. The cops know the damn score. They put the screws to every mule they get, trying to turn them—to give you up. And everybody takes the heat knowing that you'll take care of them. By now the cops have to want you bigger than ape shit. Unless you plan to give them somebody—somebody bigger than you—we got a war. They sure as shit ain't going to let you give up somebody small. The man ain't gonna be trading down."

"Well, they say you's pretty good wid dis kinda case. When it come to war they say you's the best!"

John smiled and nodded at the compliment, "They say rightly brother!" he smiled as he held out his hand.

Snappy put a large tan hand, full of rings, into his coat and came out with a bulging brown envelope. Snappy placed the envelope into John's upturned hand. John bounced it in his hand a couple of times. The envelope disappeared under John's vest.

"I don't want certain people to know that I'm gonna use you stead of they lawyer," Snappy said. "You cain't call me. I'll call you." They nodded to each other. That was it. Snappy headed back to the bar and John got into his car, parked in front of the doorway. He wondered if the bit about not using "they lawyer," meant that Snappy was ready to make a deal. A deal he would need an independent lawyer for.

Safely inside his car, he started the engine and waited until he was blocks away before he took out the envelope and looked inside. Two tightly wrapped stacks of hundred-dollar bills, side by side, each about three-and-a-half inches high. He squeezed it a couple of times and locked it in his glove compartment. "I is pretty good wid dis kind of case!" he yelled. "Of course I don't know what the fuck I'm gonna do with this one just yet, but for this kind of money I think I can spare the time to figure it out!"

As he drove on, he realized that in the morning he might ask Dick what if anything he knew about Snappy's situation, but he thought better of it. Dick might even be handling it for all he knew. He wondered if it might look bad for Dick if he was lead on Snappy's case and they went out sailing together. John decided to see if there was a point during the trip when he could mention it without getting the lecture he was sure would follow. After all, this was a real messy one. Even though his cash flow had been tight for a long while, John had quoted the fee thinking he would price himself out of it, but when Snappy set up the meet to pay the cash—oh well.

When he got home, he looked at his watch as he unlocked his front door. He was hoping Marsha was up because he wanted to tell her about the fee. He was hoping that this would make her feel better about being the wife of only a criminal law specialist. Lately, when he was not bringing in much money, he could feel her resentment that he had not stayed with corporate law. It was 2 a.m. His bed was empty. And now, after seeing the bed, there was an emptiness inside him as well.

He undressed and got into bed. When Marsha got into bed a 3:30 a.m., he pretended to be asleep. She was softly humming and he could smell alcohol and cigarette smoke on her. She didn't smoke. In the afternoon, she told him that she had accepted a last-minute invitation for them to go to a party at Karen's house. When he told her he didn't think he'd want to go, she said she was going anyway and it sounded like spite. Lately, Marsha took an almost cruel, threatening pleasure in telling him how much fun Karen was having since her recent divorce.

Marsha had grown up poor in a small town, the only child of a divorced mother. Her best friend was the daughter of a well-off corporate lawyer, and Marsha saw that as the end of the rainbow. She and John met while she was waiting tables at a restaurant near where John worked as a summer intern at the LA office of a major Wall Street firm. When they started dating, she told him that she had an eye for interior design and she wanted to pursue that as a career. They married right after John graduated, but she was disappointed that instead of corporate law John accepted a job with the Los Angeles District Attorney. John said this was a good way to get the trial experience that big firms coveted. He said that knowing your way around a courthouse is a valuable asset. If he did not like what he was doing and wanted a job with a major firm, his time with the DA would make him more marketable. She reluctantly accepted what she saw as postponement of her plan.

Marsha quit her waitress job and, even though she had no formal training, fashioned herself as an interior decorator. She had met at man at one of Karen's parties. She told him she was an interior decorator. He was a millionaire who had ties to a movie studio. She saw him as has her entrée into the world of the rich and famous. She had cards printed. She didn't know that when he flirted with her about the job, what impressed this prospective client most was not her vision for his home, which she had not yet seen, but the fact that her husband, who was talking to friends in the other room, worked for the DA. That changed one afternoon when the flirting escalated and Marsha and her new client got drunk and went to bed together. After she left, the client started to realize that the thing that attracted him to her as a connection—a husband in the DA's office—was now a huge liability. There is no good way out from an affair with a woman whose husband makes his living putting people in jail.

John found out about the Marsha's cheating on the day it happened. By chance on that day, he had a case in Beverly Hills Municipal Court. After starting the case that morning, the judge had a family emergency and put the case over to the next morning. John went home thinking he might find Marsha and surprise her by taking her to lunch. She was not home.

Shortly after finding his house empty, Karen called wanting to talk to Marsha. He told her he would give Marsha the message to call her. When Marsha got home, she seemed tipsy. He asked her where she had been. Instead of telling John she was at her client's house working, she told him she had been out with Karen. John looked her in the eye and told her that Karen called looking for her. After a long pause, she admitted to accepting a couple of drinks. And after a longer pause she admitted to having sex with "the Hollywood guy." She sobbed and said she knew it was a mistake. It had only happened that once and it would never happen again. John had to ask if she was really working for this guy—or was that a lie too. She said she was really working.

The next day, the chance of any kind of a continued relationship was doomed as soon as she told the client that John knew.

Right after that, when she came home to tell John the client said he had changed his mind about redecorating and was thinking of selling the house, John could only wonder what was true.

As he lay there waiting for her, and then pretending to be asleep to avoid any discussion of what kept her until the wee hours of the morning, he remembered finding birth control pills she hadn't told him she starting taking again after he went back to criminal law. When he found the pills, he had wondered if she was having extramarital sex or just didn't want to have a child with him if he didn't have the security of the steady paycheck from the big corporate firm. That had been a long time back but their issues around his income never seemed to be resolved.

In bed after his meeting with Snappy, as Marsha slid under the cover John was laying on top of, it was like a stranger was getting into bed with him. He felt then that they seemed to be two trains going in different directions for some time. Lying there, he couldn't remember when they were happy.

His hope of raising her opinion of his success faded. He decided to wait and not tell her about the money as she eased herself into bed. Even though he thought the money would make her happy, he was unhappy having to prove that he could make money to make her happy. He thought, It won't be being with me that will make her happy—it's the money that will make her happy. He thought, I don't think I can stand this shit anymore—more pretending. Another day of pretending I don't care what she does with Karen. Rationalizing that as long as whatever she is doing makes her happy, it's good for me. Bullshit! I don't want another day of hiding from my feelings. I can't pretend it's not what it is, it just hurts too damn much. Fuck this—if it's over it's over.

But he didn't want the confrontation this night. He knew it was something he was going to have to find time and the right moment to deal with—if there ever is a right moment—but for now he just pretended to be asleep. Then he envisioned the money locked safely in the glove compartment of his car—locked in the garage under his bedroom. Finally, he drifted off to agitated sleep.

When his alarm rang at seven in the morning, he was exhausted. He looked at the clock and tried to figure out where he was and where he had to go. He remembered his sailing date. He knew something good and something bad had happened to him last night. He thought of Marsha and the party—and the money.

As he left the house to meet Dick, he hoped they'd get back to the Marina in time so that he could put the money in a safe deposit box at his bank. He tried to remember if it was open on Saturday until three or four. There was no way in the world that he was going to deposit all of that money in his bank account. So far, because the call and meeting with Snappy had happened so quickly, he hadn't had time to tell anyone about the meeting or the money. He and Snappy were the only people who knew about it. It was too early in the morning to call his partner, Dwayne Stevenson, who everybody called Steve, and tell him about their new client and the fee. He hoped that bringing in a big fee would get Steve to lighten up. Even though John had been working and winning cases, Steve was harping that the fees in John's cases were coming in too slowly. Even with the major case John had just won, Steve complained that it was a great win for little money.

John chuckled to himself when he thought what Steve's reaction would be to Snappy's case. Both of them personally knew an attorney who called his partner in the middle of the night to tell him that he wanted to dissolve their partnership. The "next morning" a major fee case "just happened to walk in the door."

As he drove, John winced when his thoughts came back to last night and where Marsha had been. Maybe now that he had all this cash they could take some time together. He didn't like thinking that Karen's divorce was giving Marsha ideas.

Stopped at a light, he opened the glove compartment. He smiled at the money. His little secret. He'd never seen that much cash before, except for evidence in a bank hold-up case. He chuckled to himself and shook his head. He was starting to wonder what he was going to have to do to earn it when the light turned green. He closed the glove compartment, patted it once, and continued on the way to the Marina.

When he got to Marina del Rey, he could see some wisps of fog. He wondered if they would even go out. He weighed the choices. It was too early to go to the bank, but if they didn't go out or cut the trip short, he could make still make it.

He liked to go sailing. It made him feel good. He knew it always was a great escape for him. He felt that he could just let the wind blow in-one-ear-and-out the other and carry all his worries away. Sitting on a bench near the boat slip gate, he was trying his wind-trick when he saw Dick's car. When Dick got out, he was agitated.

"I'm sorry I'm late. I was just going out the door when I got a call. This guy we've been after, Snappy McNeal, was killed early this morning."

John nodded he should go on, "He and some woman. Looks like they were hit with automatic weapons and his house set on fire. Looks just like that other cartel hit two years back."

John tried not to react. For a second, he wondered if he was in any danger but couldn't see how he would be.

Dick continued, "I was in charge of prosecuting him. It was a special out of the task force. I was going to take it from beginning to end. Well, anyway the end got here quicker than we expected. Somebody saved the taxpayers a bundle. Now I got to wonder if we have a leak some-where—we were going to lock him up on Monday and somebody takes him out last night."

John tried not to reveal anything. There was really nothing to say. John thought about the woman Snappy had whispered to, he tried to visualize her sitting in the bar in her blue dress and wondered she was the woman now lying dead because she was with the wrong man at the wrong time. John could picture the envelope in his glove compartment. He'd decided he'd figure that one out later.

Dick looked at the sky. "It'll clear. Come on. Let's do it." They started unloading the boat gear from Dick's car.

Dick was his usual precise self during the preparation. In fact, he was usually a bit of a nervous Nelly about his boat, but that only lasted until they got past the breakwater. Once they were out in the open Dick would change from a pain-in-the-ass screamer to as calm a sailor as you could find.

They powered out of the Marina. Dick headed into the wind, cut the engine and set the sail once they were clear of the breakwater. Dick decided that they would head up toward Santa Monica rather than down under the LAX flight pattern. So far it was more like a drift than a sail.

Dick settled in at the tiller. He offered John some coffee from the thermos he'd brought aboard. John stared down into the hot drink while deciding to stick to his resolve and not say anything more about Snappy. It was not an easy decision. If it were to come out somehow that he was supposed to have represented Snappy, Dick would find out. John wondered how he would answer the question of why he said nothing. On the other hand, Dick was a straight arrow. He was aware that John represented the guys Dick's office was trying to put away. Now, John didn't want to deal with the disapproval. He knew that mentioning that he was prepared to take on what Dick would call "big-time-slime," would only get him a lecture. To some, handling Snappy would make John seem important. Dick would feel that John had sold his soul.

John said nothing.

After a short time watching Dick at the helm, as much to distract himself as make conversation, John decided to get his friend talking about his retirement dream. "O.K. Skipper when are you going around the world."

He knew that Dick had been planning it for quite some time. He liked to hear the way Dick spoke about it. It seemed a very well thought out dream.

"Well, as much as I love her, this little girl won't make it," he said patting the tiller of the 25-foot boat. "I've got some debts to pay off and things like that, but in about four more years I should be in a position to get the boat that will make it."

John shook his head, "Boy that would be something, if I had any idea how to sail one of these things like you can or thought I could learn. . ." he let the idea trail off. At one point John had actually thought about the freedom of sailing around the world but the more he went sailing the less the idea appealed to him.

John watched the steam rise from the cup in his hand and mingle with the fog that was starting to get thicker. The fog started to roll over the boat. The boat was starting to rock a bit. Then more than a bit. It no longer came straight down but rather the cockpit seemed to be going sideways and down. Even seated, John tried to keep his balance. At one point, he pitched toward the other side and he started to worry about going over.

Dick saw him and said, "Hang on John," as he let out the main sail a bit and reached for the foghorn in the holder on the side of the cockpit. It slipped out of his hand and fell into the cabin. "Take the tiller for a second John. Just hold her steady. I've got to get the fog horn from down below."

Through a small break in the fog, John could still see the Marina. Then that hole closed and John couldn't even see the mast.

In an instant—he thought about the money. He thought about Marsha and the troubles they were having. He used to tell her each time he paid his insurance premiums that he was worth much more to her dead than alive. Then he thought about the danger if people knew he met with Snappy. That thought was still in his mind as he hit the water. It wasn't until he felt the chill of the water that he realized what he had done. He turned around. Because of the fog he couldn't see the boat. He thought of where he had seen the land and he headed for it.

Now, on the rock, he was rested but his heart was still pounding. John knew what he had to do now. He had to look as inconspicuous as possible as he made his way to his car, to get the money and then disappear again. John thought that if he did run into anybody while he was wearing these wet clothes, he could just keep his eyes down and kind of shuffle like a homeless mental patient. If he looked like a homeless bum, it would make him invisible. He slowly walked to his car, and stifled the grin that came with the thought that he was going to be alone in the world with a year's pay in cash.

As he opened the door, he thought about fingerprints but realized from past cases that no one could tell when they were made. They probably wouldn't even check the car for prints. He was nervous. His homeless act would not wash while he was actually at the car, in fact someone who bought the homeless shuffle might think he was ripping the car off and call the police. He had to look as inconspicuous as possible —get in and out of the car fast.

He tried to get control. Hey, just slow down. Relax. It's foggy. It's early and no one is here. Besides, you haven't done anything illegal. It's no crime to be alive. He chuckled to himself, How about "swimming under false pretenses."

He saw some dry clothes in the back seat as he unlocked the car. A towel was back there. He decided not to take anything but the money. He took the envelope and slid it into his wet windbreaker. He locked up, took one last look at his car, and walked into the fog.

All he could think of was a phrase he repeated softly to himself as he walked, "—and was never heard of again."

TWO

There is a sign at the beginning of the Santa Monica freeway that says "Christopher Columbus Transcontinental Highway." John had looked at the sign for years while getting on the freeway near the Santa Monica courthouse. He loved to drive. He felt he did some of his best thinking while driving. He liked being away from his office telephone. Usually, he had his car radio tuned to an old rock- and-roll station. Sometimes he would put a tape in his car stereo and turn the sound up to block out the noise of traffic. He hated the fact that most days he had to be in several courts in several districts, and that he was under pressure to get from one court to another. But even while rushing from one end of the county to another, he felt that when he was behind the wheel he was in control of his life.

John had first noticed the sign at the beginning of Interstate 10 soon after he started his private criminal practice. He had been in Santa Monica defending a man named Frank Lots on a child molesting case. It was a particularly troublesome case. Not only did John abhor child molesting in general but, he knew that the girl involved was the same age as the judge's daughter. John had long felt that the worst crimes were those "committed on kids the age of your kids." In the client's favor was the fact that it was not a forcible crime, it was more like an offensive touching. From a legal viewpoint, the case was indefensible because the client's defense was more like a confession. From a practical standpoint, there should have been a guilty plea to a lesser charge. Since Lots was a first offender, if he pled to any charge, even with a pissed off judge, the odds were against him facing prison time. That is assuming he would come out of the mandatory psychiatric test OK—meaning he wouldn't be found to be a "mentally disordered sex offender." With any luck he was going to be put on probation. But Lots could not admit he did anything wrong. The police had Lots' story on tape. All he had said was, "She is my neighbor. Yes, I put my hand down her pants, and touched her where she said I did, but it was only the show her what not to let other men do to her."

John could not seem to convince Lots that this part of his neighbor's sexual education was not his job.

The deputy DA was loaded for bear, and the judge was making noises like he would send Lots to prison if he forced the issue to trial rather than plead guilty.

John's frustration with Lots, who seemed in all other respects to be a rational man, grew with each discussion they had about the matter. It was after one such trip out to court that John became intrigued by the sign. The trial had just been continued for the second time. This time because the investigating officer—the police officer who had put the case together and would sit at the counsel table with the prosecutor—was ill. The officer, usually a detective, would assist the prosecutor by lining up the witnesses and keeping track of the evidence, bringing the evidence, in this case the little girl's pants, to court from the police property room, until it was formally admitted into evidence. John was more than willing to continue this case. He kept looking for a way out—any way out.

Maybe Lots would die—that would be OK. Hell, maybe I'll die—that would be OK too.

After leaving court, John was just entering the freeway and thinking about the investigating officer when he realized he might have a solution to the problem. One that would end the case. He would ask that the prosecution's case be submitted on the transcript of the preliminary hearing. He would argue that doing that the little girl would not have to testify again since her testimony was already taken down by the court reporter at the preliminary hearing. John knew the prosecutor would be pushed into going along with the idea because it would save the court time and be less traumatic for the child. John could then call Lots to testify so that he could be found guilty of a lesser charge rather than plead guilty. John was sure he could get the judge to see this as almost the same as a plea of guilty, since it saved that child the trauma of being in court again, and there wouldn't be a jury trial. This way the judge might not feel that he had to send Lots to prison. John was pleased by his idea. As he passed the sign, he made a mental note to find out where the "Transcontinental Highway" went.

John found a map back at the office and saw that Interstate 10 went across the bottom of the country though places like Phoenix, Tucson, Houston, and New Orleans and ended in Jacksonville Florida.

On his next trip to Santa Monica, John proposed his disposition of the case. His client liked it because he could tell his story. The judge agreed that if the case was tried on the transcript-plus-defense, and Lots had no priors, he would not send him to prison. The DA grudgingly agreed that it would be best for the little girl and would save court time.

The case was heard that day. John was elated. He felt he had dodged a bullet. As his car rolled down the ramp onto the freeway, the air was clear and John felt he just wanted to go for a leisurely ride. But he had to be in Van Nuys. He passed the sign and said, "I haven't got time for Jacksonville today. But, some day."

It became a habit. John saw the long drive to Jacksonville as an escape from the constant ups and downs of his life. As though he would emerge on the other side of the country a new man with all ups and no downs. Whenever John went down that ramp onto the freeway, he would look at the sign and, depending on his mood, would either say softly or yell, "Someday."

Now, with his clothes still slightly damp, John was in a different car. One he had just bought for $1500 cash. He felt he had to get out of the Marina area quickly. He knew Dick didn't have a radio on the boat so John wanted to be clear of the Marina area before Dick got back to shore. After getting the money out of the glove compartment, he had made getting a car his first order of business. He hoped to find a good reliable car—nothing flashy. He also had wanted to find one with a price that someone could pay in cash and not seem out of place carrying that amount of cash on him. John saw the car on a side street right near the Marina. He had been looking for a store where he could get a throwaway-paper to check the ads for cars when he spotted it. It looked clean and had the price and details neatly printed on a sign in the rear window. It had been a simple matter, John went to the pay phone on the corner, and called the number. The owner lived just up the block from where the car was parked. After a short test ride and a short haggle over price John used the money, he had previously taken out of the envelope, to pay the man. John put the signed "pink slip" in the glove compartment. The seller was tearing up the neatly lettered sign as John drove away.

The next order of business was getting new clothes. He drove his "new car" from the Marina to the mall area not far from the Santa Monica courthouse. Normally he hated shopping. He would go with Marsha, and she had a specific idea of what he should look like and what was "in." She always wanted him to buy more clothing and more expensive clothing for himself than he felt he wanted. At the men's shop in the big department store, he noticed the way the shirts and socks were all neatly stacked and it reminded him of Marsha. She was a perfectionist when it came to neatness. His socks and clothes were always sorted and stacked and looked neater than the displays in the store. John bought his clothes; two shirts, two pair of pants, two packs of underwear, a pair of shoes, and two packs of socks.

As he tossed all of them into his new soft sided bag, he knew Marsha would have winced at the way the clothes were just dumped. The thought of never seeing her again seemed odd. He put the bag into the trunk of his car and headed for a gas station. He filled the gas tank, checked the oil and wiper fluid, checked the tire pressure and headed for the freeway. As he passed the sign, he turned up the radio, raised a fist in triumph and screamed "NOW!"

THREE

Marsha was in bed having just woken up. She looked at the clock radio. It was almost 10:30. She knew she had a bit too much to drink at Karen's and she had a headache. She was just thinking about getting up when the doorbell rang. She thought John would get it then remembered he had said something about sailing this morning. On the third ring Marsha scrambled to her feet, threw a robe over her satin nightgown, and slid into slippers on the way to the door. She grabbed her hairbrush from the dresser on the way out of her bedroom and slowed going down the long hall so that she managed to run the brush through her long dark brown hair a few times before getting to the door.

It was Dick Moran. Marsha thought he looked terrible. She started to tell him that John wasn't home but then remembered John said he was going with Dick.

"What's wrong Dick? Did John stand you up?" She moved out of the doorway inviting Dick in.

"I wish he had," he said, with a breaking voice.

Now Marsha was confused. Starting to worry, she moved across the blue-carpeted living room to the closer of the two large couches, and sat down. Dick sat on the opposite couch. The look on her face and her hand gesture asked him to say what he came to say.

"Marsha, we went out sailing. And, and John, just disappeared."

"Disappeared? What do you mean, 'Just disappeared?'"

"He was on deck when I went down to get the fog horn—the damn thing just slipped out of my hand. When I— when I got back on deck he was gone."

"Gone? What does that mean 'gone'? Gone where?"

"I mean he was not on the god damn boat when I got back on deck. Not a trace. I think I heard a splash while I was down there. But I don't know."

Marsha started shaking. She wrung her hands, "Where… where were you?"

"I'm not sure. The damn fog was really really thick. It looked like it would clear when I got down to the Marina. Damn, I should have known better. We never should have gone out. I called, I yelled. Nothing. Not a damn sound."

Tears came to his eyes and his voice got lower. She had to lean forward to hear him. "Maybe he hit his head when he went over. Maybe he hit his head on the boom and that's why he went over. I just don't know. Damn it! I… just… don't… know."

He stood up and paced in front of the couch as he spoke. "I called the police and the coast guard. They are still looking for. . . It's hard, in the fog I wasn't sure where I was." He wiped his eyes. "I had to wait till it lifted a little before I could even get back in—"

"When will someone be able to tell us something?" she interrupted.

"It's hard to say. If they find him—"

"If?"

"Marsha, it was pea soup out there. I didn't even know where to tell them to look." He sat back down heavily. His head in his hands. Marsha was getting up to go over to him when Dick realized the absurdness of her comforting him and pulling himself together, put up a hand to stop her.

There was a knock on the door.

"I called Steve from the Marina," Dick said. "I asked him and Pam to come over."

He got up and opened the door. Marsha sat on the couch shivering. At first, she felt that she was going to throw up, Then, she felt awkward with everybody in her living room dressed and her in her bathrobe like she was sick or something. Steve stopped at the doorway to whisper with Dick. Pam rushed toward her.

When Marsha saw the look of Pam's face, she thought maybe she was going to be sick after all, but got control of herself.

Pam, Steve, and Dick stayed most of the day, hovering over Marsha and making telephone calls. There was no word on John. His car was still at the Marina. Steve got a set of keys from Marsha and made plans to send an ex-cop friend to get it. Pam called Karen and she came over.

It was a long day. As it was getting dark, Steve called the Coast Guard and was told that it was getting too dark. The search was being called off. Marsha was still in her robe. It was decided that Karen would spend the night. She went home to get some clothes. Steve and Pam waited for her to get back before they left. Pam said she would be back in the morning.

Dick hung around for a while. He was a bachelor and Marsha thought he was staying just because he didn't want to go home to his empty little house. After a while, he left too.

Marsha was sitting on a couch in the living room as Karen made drinks at the wet bar near the fireplace and handed her a drink. Marsha wrapped her hands around the glass and looked into it for a long while. Karen quietly sat across from Marsha, sipping her own drink.

Marsha looked up. "What do I do now?"

"You wait."

"Wait for what?"

"You wait until they find something. You wait to find out if he's dead or just hurt. You see if there's a body. If there is, you wait until you can accept that he's dead and not going to walk in that door like he used to. You wait until you feel you can move on with your life. You wait. I know. I've been there."

Marsha looked at her slender blond friend questioningly.

Karen continued, "You knew that my first husband, Marty, was killed in Viet Nam. The hardest thing to get over there was the guilt."

She explained, "We really shouldn't have been married in the first place. We were kids."

She chuckled, "Sexually very active kids, but kids. We weren't ready to get married. We thought we would marry eventually, so when he got drafted, he figured since we talked about getting married later, we might as well get married and I could get his allotment checks. We thought we were in love and the money made perfect sense. When he went away, I began to realize that I'd made a mistake. He was the first guy I'd been with, and I guess I saw him as a way out of my parents' house. But I was going to wait until he got home to back out of it. No 'Dear John' letter from this girl. I was— Oh, Marsha how dumb of me. I'm sorry!"

"No Karen. It's OK. It's a common name and I'll be hearing it a lot. Go on."

"After I got notified that he was killed, I started to put all this guilt on myself because I wanted out of the marriage. I know I had been wishing that I wouldn't have to deal with the mess of having to tell Marty when he got back. Compared to the crap I would later be dealing with when I was divorcing Stan the telegram from the Army was a quick way out. But, when I got the telegram, I blamed myself for wishing it on him. Sounds crazy, right? Look I'm just sharing this with you because of the way you sounded lately."

Marsha challenged, "What do you mean? Ever since you and Stan hit the skids you wanted me to play around, telling me of all the rich and handsome friends your new boy friends have."

"Well, you haven't sounded too happy about the way you saw things going with you and John, and I just don't want you to fall into the trap that I did. The trap of thinking somehow you are responsible for this."

"Karen, John and I had been married for many years. We've been up and down. For a while it's been down, maybe even longer than usual but I don't think I'd wish him—dead," she said softly.

Karen went over and gave Marsha a hug. "Honey, I was warning you about the tricks we play on ourselves. I'm not accusing you. I just want you to be aware of some of what may be coming up, that's all."

After a while, they went to bed. Marsha lay awake most of the night wondering how she would manage. She tried to remember what it was like for her mother when her father died.

Her dad had owned a rare book store and died of a heart attack when she was 15. She thought back to his funeral. The sound of that first shovel of dirt hitting the top of the coffin. Then she sat up. She thought, Wait. What happens with this? If there is no body, what do we do? She started to get up and go to the guest room talk to Karen, but decided not to wake her. The morning would be soon enough for those kinds of thoughts. She finally fell asleep.

She slept late the next day. When she woke up, Karen was in the kitchen. They talked about how to proceed with services if John was not found.

Marsha also needed to admit to Karen that she had perceived correctly that things were not going well. Maybe had they continued to go downhill she and John would have broken up. She just didn't know. Karen hugged her. The unspoken words, "I apologize," were understood. They sat down and had their coffee.

FOUR

John was miles passed the Arizona State line when he saw steam coming from under the black hood of his car. He pulled to the side of the road. An Arizona Highway patrol car was heading in the opposite direction but the trooper saw the smoke and turned around. When John saw the car turn, he felt his heart jump. He told himself to relax. He had his driver's license and the signed off registration for the car. He was not going to try to get any false identification even though he had learned from a client how to beat the system.

This con artist would look through the back issues of papers and check the obituary columns for the name of someone who died early enough in life so that there would not be too many records, for example a child who was born around the time he was but who didn't live more than a year or two. Then it was just a matter of claiming to be that person and asking for a duplicate birth certificate. Usually, the birth certificates and the death certificates were not cross-indexed. Once he had a birth certificate, he could get anything else he wanted; a driver's license, a passport. Right now though John felt he would stay with who he was. That way he would not be committing any crime. He assumed that if they didn't think he was dead, the most they would do was list him as a missing person and that would not have other police agencies looking for him.

Still, he felt nervous, as he always did, when the highway patrol car put on its lights and pulled up behind his car. The officers got out. John already had the hood up.

The driver took one look under the hood and said, "It looks like you gotofflucky," and smiled. His partner shook his head.

John said, "What?"

The officer laughed at his own joke and said the words so they didn't run together. "I said, 'It looks like you got-off-lucky!' The end of your heater hose broke off from under the clamp."

He smiled, "It should be easy to just cut the end off and put the new end under the clamp." He went back to the police car and took a toolkit out the trunk, and took a switchblade knife from under the front seat. He started to make the repair.

Looking at the knife, John said, "Boy that's one hell of a throw-down weapon."

The cop looked up from under the hood. "You on the job?"

"No," said John, understanding the jargon question to mean was he a police officer, "I'm on my way East to apply for the job. Do you think I'm too old to be a cop?"

The young officer finished the fix and closed the hood. He looked at John. Then he looked at his partner who was about John's age. "Sure, you're too old. I'm younger that you are and I'm even too old to be a cop."

"There's a place to get some more water in this about a quarter mile up the road. Have a nice day."

"Thanks. Be safe." When they left John got back in the car and thought, God damn it John, get yourself under control. Why the hell were you talking cop with that guy. Let's get it together here. OK? If you are going to make it out here in the big world you had better start leaving the old language behind.

John drove up the road and put the water in the radiator. He said out loud, "Car, I sure hope you don't have many more surprises for me. But then again if they're no worse than that. . ."

As he continued heading east, he wondered how Marsha and Dick were dealing with his death. He was still angry with Marsha and thought she would be happy to be free of him but would have to hide her relief. He assumed Steve knew by now that he no longer had a partner.

John envisioned Dick, Steve and Pam, and then thought maybe even Karen, being at his house and watching Marsha play her sad new widow role.

FIVE

As John drove through Arizona that night, images of the rat race he was running from swirled in his mind. As the miles flowed under his wheels, he thought about the pure criminal law he had loved in the District Attorney's office and how he came to leave the office. He smiled as he thought of meeting his partner, Steve. He remembered his first meeting with Dick Moran. Then he thought of his friend Jerry Miyahara and what happened with Biggy Tanaka.

John and Steve met when John was prosecuting his first murder case and Steve was the investigating officer. John had prepared his case with his usual fears. He wanted to win but he was more concerned with making sure he didn't embarrass himself. Steve was an old hand, who had put himself through law school at night and was close to retirement. He acted as though he was incapable of being embarrassed. After the jury returned a guilty verdict, John realized he had a problem. He felt deep down he had just gotten a conviction on the wrong man. He watched the defendant led away in handcuffs and the defense counsel walk out of the courtroom. He saw the grief on the face of the defendant's mother as she sobbed, "He no do this. He a good son."

John asked Steve to go back to the office with him. Steve agreed without asking why. Getting to the small room that passed for an office, John closed the door behind them.

"I've got a problem. I've never had it before and I hope I never have it again. I believe the Juarez kid's story."

He saw Steve's mouth open.

John continued, "Look, I know we've been over it but I'd like to go over it one more time."

Steve shook his head and made a show of looking at his watch as he reluctantly settled into his chair. John knew Steve was patronizing him.

"OK. So, I'll owe you one—"

"Fuck that it's two," Steve interrupted. "We got the son of a bitch convicted, that's one. That's my job. Now you want to talk about getting him unconvicted. That's not my job."

John shrugged. "What do we have. We have Vinny Juarez going to see the landlord at 9 o'clock. They have an argument. We have witnesses who put him there. The next morning the same witness hears a scream and sees the landlord fall out of his second story window with a knife in his back. They go to the vic. And they see the attacker running from the scene but he's half a block away. One witness says he thinks he recognizes Vinny—the other witness isn't sure."

Steve jumps in "—and we have the lame-ass alibi that he was in a fender bender on Sunset in Hollywood while the murder was going down. He's got no back up on that. And the dirt bag ran from us when we picked him up which shows me he knows he's guilty."

"I just don't feel good with it."

"Well, I do. They don't all have to be ball-breakers. We got a fight, we got the stiff, we got no real defense and we nail the kid and put him away. One stiff one con. I like the math. They should all be this easy."

"What did you do on his alibi?"

"What the hell can you do? Go take out an ad in the paper. Did anybody see a minor fender bender at Doheny and Sunset. The kid said he hit the guy in the rear the guy looked like he was drunk and illegal and didn't want to call the cops so they just went on their way." As an afterthought Steve added, "Sunset and Doheny ain't even LAPD. That's the Sheriff's and Highway Patrol's turf. It's an unincorporated area you know."

"Yeah, I know. But the only thing is I believe this kid."

"The damn jury didn't!"

"OK, OK, thanks for your time."

John didn't want to let it rest there but he didn't know what to do. That afternoon he left for home a few minutes early and decided to drive by the scene where the kid said he had the accident. He had the feeling that he was missing something. Something obvious that he could not put his finger on. He didn't expect to find anything but it wasn't that far out of his way. John parked and got out and looked around. Right where the kid had said he had the accident there was a bank with a drive-up window.

He walked up to the girl in the glass, drive-up booth. He knew there was no way she was going to be able to remember an accident that happened several months ago and provide alibi for Juarez. He was just deciding if he should take the shot and ask her anyway when he saw TV camera and monitor.

As he stood near the glass, he could see himself and his car in the monitor. It was a long shot, but he thought, What the hell. He went into the bank and told the manager who he was. He asked how he could get to see the tapes of the day of the murder. The manager put him in touch with the chief of security. They had not yet erased that tape. The security chief played the tape for him.

There was Juarez. The numbers in the upper right-hand side of the screen put him in front of the bank at the time of the murder, just as he had said he was. John thought of the Vinny's mother. He was elated. He could hardly keep from calling Steve and telling him he told him so. John knew that he now had some technical problems but he knew they were nothing he couldn't cure. A motion by the defense for a new trial and he could lay down. He made arrangements for the tape to be saved. And went home. He knew Steve wouldn't be happy with another "unsolved" instead of a conviction but he had underestimated Steve.

Steve didn't take it badly at all. "Look, I was just doing my job. If he ain't the guy, he ain't the guy. But that was a hell of a hunch you played my friend. Maybe I should take you out to the ponies next time we go. We'd make enough so we both could retire from this bullshit."

John was relieved by Steve's reaction, pleased that there were no hard feelings. He joked "Steve, I guess your job on this one would've been easier if the murder had been in front of the camera and not the alibi."

"It sure as hell would have been," Steve smiled. "Then it would've been the Sheriff's case, that's not our turf, remember?"

John and Steve would occasionally see each other around the courthouse. Steve took his retirement and started his own law practice. His pension and some Workman's Compensation cases sent by the PBA supported him until things got rolling. John moved over to the organized crime unit where he worked with Dick Moran.

John and Dick Moran had started working for DA within a week of each other. John had come straight out of law school. Dick, a much older man, had started with the Santa Monica City Attorney's office where he worked for five years before venturing out into private practice. He'd been on his own for only four month and grabbed the job with the District Attorney's office.

John and Dick had actually met while waiting to be interviewed. The more gregarious and outgoing John noticing the somber look on the older man's face, and feeling his own tension, had struck up a conversation. After that, they always seemed to be running into each other even though they never worked together. Their training had taken them to different parts of the county, but they still saw each other after their initial orientation program.

Two and a half years after they started, they were both in the organized crime section. They, along with their boss Jerry Miyahara, formed a team, which was responsible for looking into the activities of Harry "Biggy" Tanaka.

Biggy's name came not only for his size, but from the size of the operation he controlled. This was an on-going investigation. Jerry had worked on the unit when it first started. For several years, he had been trying to get enough evidence on Biggy to put him out of business. All they could do so far was nibble around the edges, taking out some of the underlings. They had loads of information about Biggy's operation but no evidence.

No one was going to talk for the record.

Jerry would already be at his desk when John arrived in the morning and would be working long after everyone else went home. Jerry saw this not so much as a case but a crusade to rid his Japanese community of its most notorious and vicious criminal.

One morning when John arrived, he was greeted by Jerry's shouts. "We got him! That dumb Buddhahead-son-of-a-bitch finally made the big mistake," Jerry said with a raised fist.

John waited.

"Last night in a mom-and-pop restaurant in little Tokyo, Biggy was talking his shit to an importer. The guy just doesn't want Biggy to muscle in. The guy is talking very respectfully, like you would to a crazy Buddhahead shark, but he'd still saying no to having Biggy as a partner. Biggy goes wacko and shoots the guy. Pop is just coming to the table with their order and sees the whole thing!"

John just shakes his head. "You've been following this guy for how many years now? Looking for a way in. The guy's got every door locked up tight. And, then he blows his stack in a public place. What shape is the shootee in? Is he still among us?"

"He's in intensive care. A .45 to the chest will do that to you. But they say he looks good for the long haul. And, when he walks out of the hospital, I'm going to personally walk him up the center aisle of the courtroom and laugh as they drag Biggy's ass out the side door!"

"And where is our boy Biggy now," John asked.

"In and out. They picked him up at his place about an hour after the shooting. He probably had already contacted his lawyer because Biggy and lawyer were waiting outside Biggy's place when the cops arrived. They didn't want to give anybody an excuse to go in and search the house. Biggy bailed out an hour ago."

"The weapon?" John asked.

"He left it at the restaurant. He just wiped it off and put it on the table." He saw the look on John's face. "What can I tell you. I don't know what he was thinking."

Dick came in and Jerry told him the story. He looked at Jerry and John and shrugged, "I can't believe the public is paying for all this legal talent to file a straight-forward Assault with a Deadly Weapon and Attempted Murder. Maybe we should get the next kid the office hires to do this one and we move on to something else." They knew Dick was only half kidding.

While Jerry burned with his own personal fire for this case, Dick was a plodder on all cases. He did his legal thinking with a slowness and caution brought about by the self-doubt of a man who spent years in an off-brand night school that advertised in matchbook covers but still gets you to take the California Bar.

Although he always had the feeling he was beneath his younger colleagues, none of them felt that way. Dick also had a heightened sense of how what he was doing should look to an outsider. He really was concerned what the public would think. For example, it was Dick who pointed out that while they had worked on the investigation as a team and had thought that they would appear in court as a team—all sitting at the counsel table—that would look ridiculous on an ADW.

It was clear, as soon as Dick said it, that he was right. This one was going to be Jerry's. Dick would shift full time to other investigations. John would take on other assignments as well but would still back up Jerry.

At the arraignment, Jerry decided to ask the judge to increase the bail. He felt that since the victim was still in intensive care, they could still have a murder charge.

John went to watch the arraignment. He wanted to see what Biggy looked like. He got a surprise. John had seen pictures which made Biggy look shorter than he really was. The pictures also made Biggy look fat, but in court, John could tell that Biggy was all muscle.

When Biggy saw Jerry, he smiled and greeted him in Japanese. Jerry was plainly annoyed by the greeting. John knew that Jerry had mixed feelings on the race issue. While Jerry's zeal in going after Biggy was expressly because Jerry felt Tanaka was bad for the Japanese-American community, Jerry was still embarrassed to see a Japanese defendant before the court. Jerry was pleased, however, that Biggy was not represented by a Japanese attorney, he was represented by Paul Erickson an attorney known for handling mob related cases.

At the arraignment, the case was set down for a preliminary hearing. Usually set within a couple of weeks, the prelim was set for a month away to allow the victim time to recover. Jerry's motion to increase the bail was denied.

As John and Jerry went back to the office, Jerry was still brooding about the motion. "Damn Judge doesn't know what he's dealing with. Biggy is pure evil. Did you know that that son-of-a-bitch once forced a man's wife and 17-year- old daughter to act as hostesses at Tanaka's Jade House gambling joint because the man couldn't repay a loan?"

He saw the look on John's face and continued. "Yeah, that's right. Biggy has these big games and he would also have a house or an apartment for the games. This man borrowed money from Biggy. When he couldn't pay it, Biggy was making all kinds of threats. Biggy went to the guy's house one night to collect his money. He saw the guy's wife and daughter there. He told them that until the guy could repay what he owes they would have to work for Biggy at his parties for no pay. There were lots of booze at these parties and the only other people there were men."

"What the hell happened?"

"What do you think happened? The guy came up with the money after the first party. Biggy said he wanted to keep the girl there anyhow, but as soon as the as the man paid the money, he took his family and left town. They didn't want to go to the police, they couldn't live with the shame. They couldn't fight Biggy so they split."

"How long ago was this?"

"Oh, this goes back a ways, actually it probably goes back to when Biggy was starting to get his crime thing together. The idea of making an example like that is not his style now. Just like this shooting is out of character in a way.

Biggy usually gets what he wants by giving people what they want and letting them get used to it—then threatening to take it away. He prefers to get what he wants with a low profile. There is always, of course, the unstated threat—once you know who you are dealing with, you know that he is capable of anything."

Just then the telephone rang. It was Sgt. Decker, the investigating officer on the Tanaka case. Jerry took the call.

All he said was "I see," but John could tell it was bad news.

Jerry put down the telephone, closed his eyes and took a deep breath.

He turned to John, "Our victim doesn't want to testify against Tanaka. He says he wants to move back to Japan. I'm going down there to talk to him."

When Jerry got back, Dick greeted him with, "Well?"

"Nothing, I spoke to this guy for two hours. He said he just isn't going to court. He says nobody told him anything, nobody threatened him, but he's not going. Get this—he says he had just met the man who shot him outside the restaurant, and they decided to have dinner together. He never saw him before and he doesn't think he could recognize him!" Jerry slammed his file down on his desk.

John said, "Oh come on! He really said he doesn't think he could recognize Biggy Tanaka?"

Dick shook his head, "Look the guy's scared. He's been shot and he doesn't want to get the guy who shot him any angrier than he was when he pulled the trigger the first time."

Jerry said, "Well at least we have the gun and we have Pop."

"Do we have Pop?" asked John

"Yes, we have Pop," said Jerry. "I went to see him at his restaurant after I left the hospital. He says he is going to go to court. Mom is not too happy about the idea but they both know he will go. Pop says it's his duty."

Dick said, "You think he's gonna hang in there, Jerry?"

'I'm sure he will. You see he has a strong sense of duty to begin with. But, you have to add to that the fact that these people were in the camps during World War Two. While he doesn't say it, you can tell that he is going to show everybody they made a mistake when they questioned his loyalty to this country and its ideals. He'll go to court. Besides he thinks Tanaka is bad for our people, too."

"What about him going somewhere just until the prelim is over. Did you talk to him about that?" Dick asked.

Jerry grimaced, "All they have is that restaurant, they sleep upstairs. They haven't had a vacation in years. He says they'll stay and keep their place open. All the cops can do is increase the pass-bys."

As they were getting ready to go to court for the preliminary hearing, Erickson's secretary called to say he was held up in another trial late yesterday, the judge ordered him back for today, and since he's engaged in trial on another matter, he would be asking for a continuance of the hearing. She apologized for the late notice but she found the note on her desk when she got in. Jerry shook his head. He went to court to oppose the motion but they all knew the judge would grant it.

In court, John noticed that Tanaka again greeted Jerry in Japanese. This time he seemed to have more to say. Jerry didn't reply. The judge granted the motion to continue the case made by a new associate in Erickson's firm, but only put the prelim off one week.

"What does he say to you Jerry?"

"Oh, he likes to talk. I'm waiting till he gets around to my sister," Jerry grimaced.

"Your sister?"

"Yeah, my sister went to high school about a year behind him. She was the prom queen, and she says he was one bad Buddhahead then too. I'm sure he must know that she's my sister. I'm just waiting to see what he does with it."

The week passed quickly. On the morning of the prelim Jerry was upset as he came into the office.

"I really have to give up coaching this little league baseball team. My kids are getting hit with balls, knocked down at the bases, and having the worst calls you ever saw made against them. It's almost like the umpire was on the other team the way he lets them treat us."

John sat back in his chair. He knew Jerry needed to blow off steam.

"Last night," Jerry continued, "one of my kids was on first. My kid runs like he is pulling a wagon, so I'm coaching first and make sure he's got almost no lead off the base. The pitcher throws a pick-off throw over. My kid is slow but he's standing on the bag by the time the ball arrives. The first baseman knocks him off the bag and tags him. And the umpire calls him out! When I went to complain, he said he would throw me out of the game. I mean I don't know if it's racial or what. I don't think anybody would pay off an umpire to win a little league game. I tell you I got to get out of this, I hate seeing shit that's so unfair!"

Dick chimed in, "Why the hell did you get into it in the first place? You don't even have a kid."

"Well, it comes from not saying "No" fast enough. This girl I was seeing had a kid who wanted to play. I went with her to the meeting to sign the kid up. So, a guy there asks me to coach. I'm thinking about it and she goes on about how great it would be, so I kind of agreed. Two weeks later, she breaks up with me. Then I got a call from the guy in charge telling me that the season was about to start and they were counting on me. In a way I got lucky."

John asked, "Lucky, How the hell is that lucky?"

"Well, the girls kid decided he didn't want to play after all. So at least I don't have to see her and her new boyfriend coming to the games."

John chuckled, "Yeah, well I guess you could say you got lucky."

"I tell you though, I get so upset. I couldn't sleep last night. To see these poor kids pushed around like that. I can't figure what's going on. It's like a conspiracy."

The hearing was set for 9 a.m. But, when they got to court, the court was busy finishing up another preliminary hearing from the day before. Jerry met Sgt. Decker who had been in the courtroom earlier. Decker was carrying the property envelope with the gun into the courtroom. Jerry and John took Decker for a cup of coffee.

Decker told them that Mr. and Mrs. Oyama, were on call. The detective had just called them at their daughter's house. After they closed up at their restaurant, they had spent the night there because she lived walking distance to court. Decker called to tell them that they would not be needed until about 11:30 because they were starting late.

At 10:30 they went back to the courtroom. They were ready to proceed at 10:45. Jerry's first witness was the of-ficer who responded to the scene and recovered the gun. Jerry took the gun out of the envelope and showed it to the officer. After a cross-examination that seemed to Jerry to be pure nit picking, Jerry offered to stipulate that the ballistics expert would testify that the bullets from this gun matched the bullets taken from the victim. To Jerry's surprise and the judge's obvious annoyance, Erickson re-fused the routine stipulation. He wanted to cross-exam-ine the expert witness. Jerry got a five-minute recess and had Sgt. Decker call the Oyamas to tell them that they wouldn't be needed until after lunch while Jerry called the crime lab and told the ballistics man to come on over.

Jerry put on the expert and his direct examination was short and to the point. Jerry took the gun off the table in front of him and showed it to his witness. Yes, that was the gun he had test fired. And, yes, the bullet taken from the victim and the one he test fired matched. Cross-examination seemed to be just a big fishing expedition, with questions being asked over and over again. At one point, the judge felt that it was necessary to remind Erickson that this was only a preliminary hearing. When that witness was excused, they broke for lunch.

Jerry and John, back at their office, were halfway through their lunch, and trying to figure out why Erickson seemed to be stalling for time, when the call came. It was Sgt. Decker.

The Oyamas were dead.

Decker came over and took Jerry to the scene. Jerry was sickened by the blood. Mr. and Mrs. Oyama were in one bedroom. The old man had been shot in the mouth. His wife had been shot in the back of the head. The daughter was on the floor in the other bedroom along with her daughter who had just come home from school for lunch. They had also been shot in the back of the head. Jerry fought back the tears as he looked at the little girl. But he couldn't contain himself when he saw her braids covered in blood.

He looked at his watch to get himself back under control. He gritted his teeth as he told Decker it was time to go back to court. With their main witness laying on the ground in front of him, Decker wondered what it was going to be like in court, but he just shrugged and agreed to drive Jerry back.

Tanaka and Erickson where already near the counsel table when John met Jerry and Decker at the courtroom door. He could see that Jerry was shaken. Jerry couldn't look John in the eye. He stared past him to the defense side of counsel table. John put both hands on Jerry's shoulders. Without saying anything, he was asking Jerry if he was OK. Jerry looked at John, took a deep breath, nodded to John, and walked to the counsel table. John, as he had done whenever he was in court as spectator, took a seat in the back of the courtroom.

Tanaka and Erickson were just sitting down at the counsel table when John noticed Jerry take the property envelope from Sgt. Decker. He saw Jerry move around to the front of the counsel table into the well of court—between the counsel table and the judge's raised bench with the attached witness stand.

Jerry put the gun on the table, where it had been during the morning, as though he were going to proceed with the hearing. For a second John thought that Jerry was denying to himself that his witness was dead.

Then in a quick motion Jerry had the clip with the bullets out of the little envelope where it was kept to separate it from the gun. He took a step back from the counsel table and rammed the clip into the gun.

Tanaka saw him first—his attention drawn by the click-sound of sound of the gun being loaded, followed by the clacking sound made when Jerry pulled back the slide to engage a bullet. As Tanaka stood up, Jerry took a step to his left to face him across the table and pulled the trigger. The shot hit Tanaka on the bridge of his nose and sent him and his chair flying backwards. The next shot caught Erickson behind his left ear as he tried to dive under the counsel table.

Jerry looked at Decker and the bailiff in the back of the courtroom. He saw Decker start to get up. It seemed that Decker and Jerry made eye contact for an instant. Then Decker sat down again and placed his hands out in front of him palms down on the table. The bailiff in the back took a step but stopped and kept his arm folded.

Jerry raised the gun to his own head, took a step back away from the counsel table, and fired.

The whole scene took only seconds but it seemed to John to go by in slow motion. John, started to get out of his seat, and was half-standing when Tanaka was shot. He was on his feet and starting to rush to Jerry but stopped when he saw Jerry fall backwards and the splash of his blood and brain on the front of the raised bench. He knew Jerry was dead. From where he stood, John could also see the spreading blood coming from Tanaka and Erickson. He went back to his seat and sat down.

The sound of the shots brought bailiffs and other police officers, who were in the building, pouring into the court with guns drawn. Word of what had happened quickly spread though the building. When Dick Moran heard, he went to the courtroom—pushed his way in.

Dick found John where he was crumpled and crying in the back of the courtroom, and led him, in silence, back to their office.

Later, when John was questioned, he could describe each movement he had seen as though it happened in a movie he had just watched over and over. He was sadly surprised that what had taken so few seconds to transpire took so long to describe. As he thought of how quickly the whole thing had happened, he began to reproach himself for somehow not knowing Jerry was not OK. He reproached himself for somehow not getting to Jerry in time to keep him from killing himself. But, rationally, he knew there was no way he could have gotten from the back of the courtroom to Jerry in the short time it took for the event to unfold. He could not convince himself that there was nothing he could have done.

After Jerry died, John took two weeks leave and thought about his priorities. He liked Jerry but Marsha had never met him. They had never socialized because Jerry wasn't married. John realized that much of his social set was people like he and Marsha that he had let Marsha pick.

John decided he was going to leave the DA's office and get out of criminal law. Marsha was delighted. She looked forward to John working for more money with one of the big firms that were eager to hire ex-DA's with trial experience.

John also decided that he wanted to retain his friendship with Dick, his only non-married friend. There was a tacit understanding between them—neither wanted to talk about Jerry. John called and got himself invited out on Dick's boat. John was aware enough about his situation to kid Dick that the only other way for them to get together—other than at Dick's annual Christmas party— was for Dick to remarry. Dick laughed and said he'd rather go sailing.

John wanted to open up his life a little more. He saw the change in jobs and making time to go sailing with Dick as the way to do that.

At first, Marsha resented his spending time with Dick. She thought he should cut his ties with the old job completely. She seemed to resist almost any change unless it was shown to be totally to her advantage. But John wasn't prepared to cut himself off from his past completely as he looked for the kind of firm Marsha thought he should want.

Now, as John drove, he had tears in his eyes as he always did when he re-lived that day with Jerry in the courtroom. John's neck and shoulders ached and he knew he had to get some sleep.

SIX

Approaching Las Cruces, New Mexico John was tired. He knew he had better get off the road. He thought about a motel but wasn't sure how to register. He wondered if he'd have a problem registering in motel without a credit card.

He found a place that had a big sign just off the road that called itself an economy motel. It looked like it was clean, not too expensive and just out of the way enough. He took his credit cards out of his wallet and put two hundred-dollar bills in. He put the rest of the cash in his soft-sided bag and went in.

When the clerk asked him how he was going to pay for the room, John said he would pay in cash and asked if he needed some money in advance. The clerk said he would need to be paid in advance and needed a hundred-dollar deposit.

John filled out the registration card. He used his own name but wrote in a handwriting no one could read. He was in his room and asleep in minutes.

As the sight and sound of interstate traffic went by his room, John had a dream. It was more a nightmare. He was at a party at someone's home. There seemed to be a lot of well-dressed pretty people around. Most of the people where John's age. Everybody seemed to be having a good time. There was a lot of laughter and music. Everyone, including John, had a drink in his hand.

He was having a conversation with an older man and realized in the dream the man was wearing a judge's robe. The man smiled as John spoke with him. He was interested in John and listened intently. John was telling him about a major case that he had won.

Just as John was getting to the end of the story, the judge was approached by a beautiful woman. She stood about 5 feet from the judge and waited until he saw her. When he saw her, he moved toward her. She let him approach until she was just out of his reach and then she backed away. She smiled and kept backing herself just out of his reach. John put his hand on the judge's arm and tried to hurriedly finish his story. He wanted to tell the glory part. The girl kept backing up and luring the judge away. When she got to the front door of the house, she turned and glided to a big black car that was waiting for her. The judge nodded to the hostess as he went down the steps and into the back seat of the car. John was running along after the judge and trying to finish his story and trying not to spill his drink as he ran. Then the drink wasn't in John's hand. He was fumbling around trying to find his card. People came out of the house and stood on the steps to watch as John was trying to finish his story and squeeze his card into the rolled up back window of the car as it sped away.

John woke up in a cold sweat. He lay there for a few seconds trying to figure out where he was. The roar of the trucks on the interstate told him. Then he remembered how he had gotten there. He looked at his watch it was 2:44 a.m. He checked on the money. Still there. He tried to fit the pieces of the dream together.

The judge looked a bit like his partner, Steve. Maybe older than Steve but it could have been him. He didn't recognize the girl at all. The place where the party was looked familiar but he couldn't quite place it. He thought about it for a while. It bothered him. Then he remembered. The setting in the dream looked like the house of Hartford Boggs. He had been there at a party. From that party John started on the road back to criminal law.

John had left the DA's office to work for a large civil firm that wanted to expand their litigation department. It was a branch of a heavyweight national firm with an office in Century City. Several of the members of the firm were into national politics. A few of the partners had been either Senators or in the legislature and carried that influence with them. One was a campaign manager who had run and won a presidential campaign.

John had been with the firm 8 months when he and Marsha had been invited to a party at the home of Hartford Boggs, the managing partner. Unlike the party in the dream though, this party was a sit-down dinner. There were about 15 couple seated around a huge formal dining table. Marsha and John were easily the youngest people there.

He was wondering why he was at this party. He was telling a smiling, gray haired woman that he had just heard from a friend who had won a case in the Court of Appeal. He realized as he was talking that other people were starting to listen to the story. John had thought it was a good joke.

He had run into a friend of his from law school. John had just left the District Attorney's office and had two weeks before he was due to start with this firm. The friend told John that he had just gotten a criminal appeal that had a lot of money riding on it. He knew nothing about criminal law but felt to keep the client he had to take this case. The opening brief was due in a week and he hadn't even started on it. He asked John for help. John ghosted the brief for him before starting with the firm. He thought nothing more about it.

John laughed, "Yesterday my friend called to tell me he submitted on the brief, so he would not have to go and embarrass himself at oral argument, and he won."

The gray-haired lady smiled at John's story. Marsha seated across from them was not as happy with the outcome as John. "I told John that he shouldn't do things like that unless he gets credit for them. The case made all the papers and this other lawyer is making a name for himself. Sometimes John is like a little boy. He thinks it's a great joke that his friend won a huge case he knew absolutely nothing about."

John glared at Marsha. He wanted her to keep her dissatisfaction for a less public place. Boggs, seated at the head of the table, had listened to the story. "John, we should talk about your criminal law experience on Monday. I was approached this afternoon by Mr. Johnson, he has cleaned our offices for nearly twenty years. He and I spent plenty of nights together in that office. He came to me for advice." He started to go further then looked around the table and thought it would be improper. "Let's talk about it on Monday morning."

John nodded his agreement.

On that Monday John was at Hartford Boggs's door.

"John, as you know we try to give some thought around here to pro bono work for the less advantaged. Mr. Johnson has come to me and we would like to try to help him in this matter. It seems his son was arrested for possession of a dangerous weapon. We would like you to represent him."

"In the firm's name?"

"Yes, of course. See what you can do."

John spoke to Mr. Johnson that evening and saw his son, Reggie, at the jail the next day.

The day after that he appeared at the arraignment. It felt strange being on the opposite end of the counsel table. The deputy DA in the courtroom seemed young and cocky. He looked at the firm name on John's card.

"This is a pretty straight forward case," he said as he handed John the police report, "not much you can do with that." John thanked him and looked at the police report and the copy of the complaint attached to it.

He went through the arraignment ritual with his client and waived a formal reading of the charges and got the bail reduced to an amount the Johnson's could pay.

Back at the office, John made copies of the police report and the complaint and dictated a memo as to how he had spent the morning. He took the photocopies he had just made and went to see "the boss."

"How does it look?"

"Well, the police report is kind of sketchy but they keep them that way. I once overheard a cop tell a rookie to keep as much information as he could in his head because it was more flexible that way."

Boggs shook his head.

"This is set for preliminary hearing in ten days. We'll find out more about it then. It may be that we can win it then but that's hard because the standard of proof is so low. I've already explained to the Johnsons that all that is needed at the preliminary hearing is for the People— all cases a filed in the name of the People of the State of California—to generate a reasonable suspicion that a crime was committed by the defendant and the magistrate will bind the defendant over for trial in Superior Court. Reasonable suspicion is a far cry from proof beyond a reasonable doubt."

Boggs looked over his glasses at John, "We feel comfortable that the Johnson matter is in good hands. Good luck."

John took the comment for the dismissal it was and went back to his work.

The preliminary hearing had been set for a morning but was trailed over to the afternoon. John had to run back to the office and dictate that he had spent the morning watching the judge hear four other prelims, handle several arraignments and give out a few sentences. Watching the other prelims told John that he had a judge who knew what a reasonable doubt was. He was not a rubber stamp that would bind everyone over to Superior Court. John felt that if there was a chance for his client, this judge would give it to him.

At one thirty, John was back in court and the case was set to go. When he arrived, the clerk told them that she was transferring the case to the Commissioner down the hall. John went down the long hall to the other courtroom with the Johnsons. He saw the Public Defender in the courtroom and introduced himself.

"What do you know about this guy?" John asked.

"He binds everybody over."

It was the answer John was hoping not to hear.

"Well," said John I guess I'm not going to be popular with the clerk but I'm not going to stipulate to this guy."

John explained to Mr. Johnson and his son what was going on. "The Commissioner here is not a judge. We are entitled to have a judge hear our case. The Commissioner can only hear it if everybody agrees to let him hear it.

Since I think we have a better chance with the judge we just came from, I'm not going to agree to let the Commissioner hear the case."

As John expected, the clerk was not happy. John told her he was not going to blow his client's chance to avoid having to stand trial in Superior Court. She made her displeasure clear as she took the file back from John. She made a show of putting it at the bottom of the stack. She hissed "Mr. Street, you are aware this is a weapons prelim." And in a lower whisper through clenched teeth, "What the hell do you think you're going to do with a weapons prelim?"

John just shrugged and walked away. But he looked to see if she was going into chambers to spread the bad word. She didn't have a chance. Just as John sat down a buzzer sounded twice and that was the signal that the judge was coming out of his chambers.

John sat through the rest of the calendar but was impressed that the judge took no breaks and just kept working. At 3:45 the judge got to their case. The judge asked if both sides were ready and both sides announced that they were. John noticed that there was only one police officer left in the courtroom and he was holding the alleged dangerous weapon. It was the nightstick, which under the dangerous weapon section of the Criminal Code would be called a "Billy club."

Reggie had told John he had cleared out of his locker when he was laid off by a private security guard company and put the club in the back of his car under his old uniform shirts and pants. From the police reports, John knew they would need two cops to prove their case. The first office who stopped Reggie's car and the other one who found the nightstick in the back seat under the uniform which Reggie would no longer be wearing.

John sat down and waited.

They called the officer to the stand and he described how he came upon Reggie's car after it had been stopped by another officer and when he looked into the back seat, "There in plain sight was this illegal Billy club."

Reggie leaned over to tell John that the officer had opened the back door of the car and had to go rummaging under the content of the locker to find the nightstick underneath.

John listened and made a sign with his hand to tell Reggie to stop, he understood.

When the officer finished the judge looked at John who, to the surprise of everyone except the judge, said he had no questions.

When the DA moved to have the Billy club received in evidence, John said. "Objection, Your Honor, I move to suppress the evidence. This officer arrived at the scene after the defendant's vehicle had already been pulled over and there has been no testimony from which the you can conclude the original stop was lawful."

The judge smiled and agreed. The DA sputtered that he wanted a continuance to call the other police officer. Looking at John, the judge said, "Counsel?"

John shrugged and shook his head.

"Your Honor, the Court asked if both sides were ready and both sides said they were. We all proceed in good faith in reliance on those representations. Now we are being asked to allow the DA to claim he wasn't ready after all and he wants a do-over. I think he is estopped from taking that position now."

The judge smiled at the DA.

"In case they didn't cover the law of estoppel in your prestigious law school. When you make a statement or do an act that someone in good faith acts on—they are relying upon that statement or act— you will not be allowed to change your mind.

Mr. Johnson had a right to one preliminary hearing. You said you were ready for it, and now you want him to have two. Nice try."

He nodded to John, "Case dismissed."

"Thank you, Your Honor," John got up and shook hands with his client. He noticed that the clerk was not at her desk any longer. Mr. Johnson, the white-haired old janitor limped over with tears in his eyes, and said, "His Momma will be so happy he's coming home!"

John shook hands all around again and left. When he got outside, he was tired but pleased. He felt the tension in his neck. He tried his trick of thinking of the wind blowing through his ears to take the headache away.

He headed back to the office to dictate the results. He was annoyed that he had to button his collar button and straighten his tie before entered the building. At his desk, he looked at the mound of paperwork. He knew that it would be months before he did any meaningful trial work for the firm.

He started to think about his situation at the firm, and think about the feeling he had in the courtroom today. He looked at his buttoned-up self in the mirror. He knew how lost he felt doing civil law.

Over the weeks and months, that feeling, of being lost in the civil law, grew and he started to think he should go back to criminal law.

Now, John lay in his bed near Las Cruces and thought of how he had run back to criminal law. How he had heard that Steve now had a growing criminal practice and needed help.

Marsha hated his decision to leave the Boggs firm. She liked the people at the firm and she liked the wealth and social status of clients that the firm represented. She felt that John's years in the DA's office were supposed to be the fast route to the trial experience that the big firms wanted. Becoming a criminal defense lawyer was not supposed to be for a man with a wife, who said he wanted a family. She did not want to ride the income roller coaster that came with being self-employed and representing criminals. Marsha felt that before they could have children John needed to be working at what John, himself had called the "big buck firms."

Without any discussion, Marsha went back on birth control pills.

Marsha had insisted that John finish the year with the Boggs firm. She told him that anything less than a year any place would look like he was irresponsible to anyone seeing his resume. She was hoping too that John would change his mind and stay with Boggs, or that Steve would not be able to wait. But John was able cover for Steve on a few occasions to help him out. Usually, it just meant going to one court and asking to continue the matter Steve had in that court to another date because he was tied up in another court. John also used these brief visits to the criminal courts to let people know that he would be working with Steve in about three months.

After going into criminal defense work, he knew, in terms of building his own practice, he was going to be sucking up to judges and clerks to get appointments to handle the indigent defendants that the public defender's office couldn't handle because of conflict of interest. John knew he couldn't depend on Steve always bringing in the business. And Steve wouldn't want him to. John needed the bread-and-butter work until he got the reputation that would cause the bigger boys—the crooks for whom crime did pay—to look him up. But then too, he still had to know the judges. Some he had known while he was a DA, but he felt he had to keep his face in front of them. He had to know the people who would decide the fate of his clients' and his own career. John knew that had he been appointed to represent Johnson it would have been a very risky decision to defy the clerk by not stipulating to the Commissioner. She would see his actions as biting the hand that fed him. If he was going to get along, he had to play the game.

Now in his motel bed, John starred at the ceiling and was wondering what was happening back at home when he fell back to sleep.

SEVEN

John and his partner, Steve, had their offices in Hollywood. It was on the second floor of what looked like a mass-produced office building. There were several just like it in the area. Each had a bank on the first floor, across the lobby from the bank would be a hole-in-the-wall snack counter, and near the snack counter there would be a door with big gold lettering spelling out the name of either a record company which no one ever heard of or film company which no one ever heard of.

Steve's office was done in dark colors and had a huge desk that looked like a mahogany boomerang complete with a built-in telephone. On the walls, he had framed old newspaper front pages, the headlines announcing an arrest or killing, all of which memorialized Steve's days with the Los Angeles Police Department.

John's office was down the hall near the library. Even though Marsha was not happy with John's return to criminal law, she took on the task of decorating his office the way she thought a successful lawyer's office should look. It had a modern looking desk with chrome and fabric chairs in front of the desk for clients. Behind the chairs was a matching couch separated from the chairs by a see though glass topped table. Her one concession was to John's desire to have a high back leather chair.

Two days after John's disappearance, Steve was at John's desk sorting through John's files. Steve hated paper work even more than John did. Steve was doing what he knew he should have done the day before, trying to get a handle on those cases that needed something done immediately. He was up to the C's when he heard his phone ring. Steve went back to his office to take the call from Dick Moran.

"Steve, I don't want to bother Marsha about this but I need a picture of John. The only one I have is at last year's Christmas party at my house and your arm is cutting off half of John's face."

"There's one on his desk with Marsha in it but you can see him clear enough. Somebody can come pick it up. Dick, what is going on?"

"Maybe nothing. Maybe something. The task force is out on this Snappy McNeal killing. The girl with him was a pro. I guy from administrative vice says she used to work out of a pimps-and-players joint on the boulevard up near you."

"Yeah, I know the place. I raided it myself once. Who's the guy from ad vice," Steve asked wondering if he knew him.

"I don't remember, I've got it here somewhere if it's important. Anyway, the deal is that the task force guy goes up to this place and talks to the bartender. And, 'Yes' Snappy had been in that place that night and yes, he left with the girl, but the guy says that Snappy came in and looked over to a white dude who looked out of place wearing his three-piece suit. From the description it could be John."

Steve's ex-cop mind raced ahead. "I don't know why John would up there talking with Snappy, but if this guy can put John in the bar with Snappy, we might have a winner! Maybe whoever done Snappy…"

"Steve we're just running down leads as to why Snappy got hit and this John thing popped up. We don't have any kind of angle at all yet."

"Well, I do," Steve interrupted, "it's called insurance. Marsha and I each have a policy for one million dollars on John's life. Mine is a key man policy, John had one on me to. In fact, they were his idea. If he can't be found we have to wait seven years to collect, because there's no body. If we can show he was exposed to a known risk we can collect now. Being out on a small boat in the fog may or may not be the kind of risk we need, but now we've got this Snappy deal."

Dick was getting annoyed, "Maybe I'm a little slow this morning, what exactly have you got?"

"Snappy was a big dealer, hell, he was one of the Magnificent Seven, and stop me if I'm wrong but, I'm guessing you and the task force guys had made it up the ladder as far as him but no higher, right?"

"Go on," said Dick, neither confirming or denying.

"So, the only way you're going to get above Snappy, and get everybody else, is through Snappy. So, he's taken out. If the guy in the three-piece suit is John, whoever took out Snappy, sees the lawyer Snappy talks to go out sailing with the guy who is prosecuting the case."

Dick just listened.

Steve continued. "They know Snappy's only way out is to give somebody up. And they figure Snappy told John who that somebody was."

"You know, you might've been a cop too long."

"OK, shoot it full of holes. I know that the guys holding the insurance money, that they do not want to pay out, are sure going to try."

"We don't even know that John was talking to Snappy. Unless he told you something about it."

"No. But what the hell is John doing in this hooker bar."

"Hey, slow down. We don't know it's John in the bar. Then we don't know if he was there to talk to Snappy. If Snappy gives John any names—and how the hell do they make the hit. I didn't hear anything near us in the water. You could hardly see your hand in front of your face out there, Steve. The LAPD best SWAT guys couldn't have hit John in that soup. When I came on deck, I couldn't even see the water when I looked down—damn fog was so thick I didn't know where the hell we were. For your theory to work they had to hit him with a shot that made no noise and knocked him off my boat clean because there was no blood. And it would be easier if they took us both out—blow up the boat or something rather than this far-fetched miracle shot you're talking about. Man, I doubt if this one will fly, Steve. Lord knows I'll help all I can, it's the least I can do. But, trying to sell this one…"

"Well, we'll see. Hey, I wish John were here and he could wade through his files. I wish this whole damn thing never happened. I'm too old to handle this crap alone again. We have to make the best of a shit deal."

"Steve, if he was the guy in the bar, being out that late maybe he was tired and just lost his balance. I don't know. He didn't look really tired. Anyway, I told him about Snappy getting hit and he didn't say a word. Not a damn word. So, I just don't know. I'll send someone for the picture. We'll run it under the bartender and see if we even have that much. I'll get back to you."

"OK."

"In the meantime, Steve, are you going to help Marsha with some arrangement for some kind of service or something. Does she have enough money to live on for a while?"

"Her money is OK for now. I had Pam check on that. She's over there again today. Pam says Marsha's hanging in there. I'll go over and check on things when I get out of here tonight."

"Thanks Steve. I'd go but I feel partly responsible and don't think they'd want to see my face."

"Hey, Marsha said yesterday she hoped you didn't blame yourself for this."

"Well, I shouldn't have gone out."

"Hey Richard! Don't do that. John was a big boy. He could see the weather just as well as you. If he didn't want to be on the damn boat, the only thing that could have made him go was either a court order or Marsha."

Dick thanked Steve for trying to make him feel better and said he'd send someone to the office for the picture.

The next day Dick called back "It was one of those things, Steve. You know how they go. The bartender isn't sure it's John. One of the girls there is sure it is, and two others are just as sure it's not."

"Well, we may have a break on our end anyway. Right after your investigator, what was his name, Robinson? picked up the picture, Manny Schwartz from upstairs came down to kind of pay his respects, to offer to help out, you know. He and I started talking about this insurance angle, he does a lot of civil stuff. It's his whole practice. It also turns out that Manny used to represent the company until they went to an in-house-counsel-set up, but his brother is in charge of that.

"Anyway, he made some calls over there. Nothing final yet, but they might look for a soft spot to lie down on this one rather than give us a hard time."

Dick exhaled slowly, "Boy that would be a blessing. But I never heard of an insurance company looking to come across with two million bucks without some kind of struggle."

"OK, I agree, but Manny reminded me of the time that John and I once helped him on a criminal case, a possession of drugs. The girl we helped was the daughter of the guy who owns the damn insurance company we have the policy with. Manny brought me the case just before John started here. It was maybe a year before we bought the policy. Anyway, the girl had gone out with this guy and didn't know he was into drugs. It was like their second date. So, she lets him drive the new car she got as a graduation present from Daddy and they get stopped by a black and white unit for rolling through a stop sign."

"CRS," said Dick, "Ye old California rolling stop."

"Yep. So, the bulls exit the black and white," Steve continued, "and one who's goes up to the boyfriend on the driver's side, while his partner takes his position behind the car, and the partner sees this guy hand our girl an envelope and he hears the guy say, 'Get rid of this,' to the girl. The partner reaches in and takes it from her hand. The envelope has felony-weight stuff.   The girl's got no record, but it's her car and the stuff is in her hand. The boyfriend is a real dirt bag and he's telling the girl she is going away unless she has her dad make his bail and pay for his lawyer and blah blah blah.

"Well, I get the case and make sure they get separate trials. The case is set for trial on the same damn day

John comes on board here. I figure it ain't fair to stick John with a trial his first day. But I'm running around to three different courts, so I figure John should just go out and continue it for me. John goes out to the court and the damn judge won't let him continue it.

"So, John has to put the case on. So, John waives jury and convinces the judge that the girl has no knowledge of drugs. She didn't know what was in the envelope and that the cop had her as soon as the envelope is in her hand. John argues that that is not the kind of possession and control that the law was intending to prohibit." Steve laughs, "The judge buys the argument and finds her not guilty."

Dick said, "That sounds like the bit John pulled with me once. It was just before he started with you. I was out in the boonies. I don't remember why the hell I was even there. They didn't have a City Attorney or something and I wound up putting on their traffic calendar. Anyway, John came out to meet me for lunch and he's sitting in the visitor's section waiting for me to finish. They had a lawyer sitting as a judge that day and he calls the case of some kid. The judge takes one look at this kid and says he doesn't want him to represent himself. The judge looks around the courtroom and asks if there are any lawyers in the court who would assist. I fingered John for the job. He takes the kid aside for two minutes and announces that he is ready for trial. It was a real biggie, a major crime if there ever was one," Dick chuckled. "The kid was charged with failure to proceed through the green light."

"What? What asshole wrote that chicken shit ticket?"

"Some highway patrol guy. He got up there and testified that he and his partner were watching the kid and his buddy talking to some girls in another car and when the light turned green the kid did not go through the intersection."

"That was it?"

Dick said, "That was it,

"But of course, you have to add the formula-testimony elements that the kid's car did not seem disabled, you know the hood wasn't up, stuff like that."

"Of course," Steve chimed in, sounding just as sarcastic as Dick had.

"John asks the cop a couple of questions and calls the kid as a witness. The kid says he was lost and his friend was asking the girls for directions but he didn't talk to the girls at all. When the light turned green, he went through it."

John argues to the judge that he has now heard two versions of how soon after the light turned green the kid went through it. He adds with a little bow toward the CHP guy that he means no disrespect but just because he is a cop doesn't mean he perceives the change from red to green or the passage of time any better than his defendant does. Since the case has to be proved beyond a reasonable doubt, a doubt means the defendant wins.

"The judge smiles and says he has used that argument too many times himself in defense of clients not to agree with it now. He finds the kid not guilty. Then he apologizes to John that he, only a lawyer acting as a judge, can't order some compensation for John accepting the appointment. John just waived him off."

Dick laughs, "Then John leans down to me and tells me since I lost I could buy lunch."

"That's John all right," Steve said. "And he had no concept of money. One time some guy in the building stopped him and asked him if he would handle a drunk driving case. John had just handled one for some probation officer he knew for $500. I told John to let me do the talking and we went upstairs to the office of the guy who wanted John to handle his case. It was the guys second DUI. The guy was wearing a $2,000 suit with custom made shirt and sitting behind a $10,000 desk. I told the guy we needed $5000 and the guy wrote a check without blinking an eye. John would have handled the damn case for $600 thinking he gave his probation office buddy a $100 discount!"

"Well," Dick continued, "In the one he handled for free, the kicker was that the highway patrol guy was really pissed off. I mean he turned red and went storming out of the court. I felt sure he'd be looking for John on the road back. But—" Dick realized they had been talking a long time. "Whoa! I've got to get going here. I have to get back to what they are paying me for. Have you said anything to Marsha about any of this insurance stuff?"

"No, I think it's much, too soon. Besides nothing is set yet. And I'm still trying to get John's stuff squared away. No disrespect intended, Dick, but he sure must have had a hell of a memory because there isn't a lot of documentation in his files."

"Well, I guess none of us really prepares them thinking someone else will need to finish them, even though that was his training in the office here. Just keep me posted OK? I've got to go."

Later that day, after Steve spoke to Manny Schwartz again, he felt he had enough to tell Marsha. He went to see her to explain about going to court to have John declared dead. She asked if Steve thought when the court ruled that that would be a proper time to have a memorial service. Steve agreed it would be. He explained the whole plan to her. Even though the stakes were high, the insurance company would not put up too much of a fight. "The man whose daughter John had helped was in fact in a position to return the favor so to speak. Also, Manny was able to supply us some input: the insurance company wanted to look good to lawyers because it was starting to expand its business in the area of structured settlements."

Steve explained that a structured settlement occurs in big personal injury cases. He looked to see if she was following. No matter, all she really needed to know was what Manny thought—for business reasons, the company they had their policies with didn't want look bad by hassling a lawyer's widow.

"So," Steve explained, "we have to wait a while, maybe a few months, but when the time comes it looks like they won't fight too hard. We still have to go to court to have the court declare John dead, but we may have an in there too. Red Davis is sitting as a probate judge. He's my old partner from the job. If I can maneuver the case in front of him…"

Steve did not think it necessary to go into more detail with Marsha about his relationship with Red Davis. They had been partners when they worked robbery-homicide years ago. When Steve started going to law school at night, he convinced Red that he could do it too. Red graduated a year after Steve did. Steve had passed the bar but still had a way to go to retirement. Red was due to retire about six months after he took the bar. Steve stayed up at nights with Red to help Red pass the bar. Red was always into political stuff so when he retired, he knew that as soon as he put in the minimum time as an attorney he would be appointed to the bench. It was one day before Red's retirement that Steve saved Red's life.

Red had put in his twenty years and was set to go to work for a firm that handled a lot of the policemen's workman's compensation matters.

It was late in Red's last day that they got a call to assist a patrol unit in the area they happened to be in. The black and white unit was chasing a man from an armed robbery. Steve knew that they had to respond to the call, but with Red's time so short, he drove as slowly as he could. While he didn't like to hang up the cops at the scene, he hoped that the action would be over by the time they got there. When they arrived at the scene, the uniformed officers in front of the building said their guy went in. They had another unit coving the back and the guy was still in there but they didn't know which apartment he was in. Steve and Red both recognized the building as one where they had arrested a bank robbery suspect two months before. They checked the description of the suspect with the uniformed officers. The description and the recital of how he had jumped over the teller's cage screaming, stuffed whatever bills he could grab into a paper bag, and ran out screaming, led them to feel sure it was the man they had arrested before. His apartment was on the second floor near the back stairs. Red, saying he wanted this guy as his last collar, started up the stairs. Steve couldn't let Red pull such a macho stunt. He raced past Red on the stairs and hit the door to the apartment in full stride.

The suspect, alongside the door with his shotgun held head high, didn't react fast enough. Steve was moving so fast that he was through the door and past the suspect by the time the shotgun fired. Steve turned as he was going to the floor in the room and the shot from his service revolver hit the suspect in the chest. Steve knew that if Red had gone up to the door, in a deliberate manner, he would have taken the shotgun blast through the door.

Now Steve, whether he could show John was in the bar with Snappy or just fell off the boat, was planning to maneuver the probate matter in front of his old buddy. With the insurance company not prepared to make a fight of it, Red Davis was all that stood between Steve and the biggest payday he had ever thought of.

EIGHT

John saw the woman for the first time as he was pulling in at a rest stop in New Mexico. She was tall in her high heels and wearing a tight silvery jump suit. He thought it was one heck of an outfit. By the time he parked, she was in her Trans-Am and gone. He noticed she drove off alone. He wondered who she was and where she might be going, but that was all. He went to the men's room, came out, and got coffee and a doughnut from a charity organization that was doing a fund-raising project, donated a couple of dollars, and got on his way.

It was just after dark when John spotted the car with the girl up ahead. She was at the side of the road with a highway patrol officer. He had his book out. John wondered if she had really been speeding or the cop just wanted to get to know her better.

A little while later, she went flying by him. Instinctively John looked at his speedometer. Even though he promised himself he was going to stay a legal 65 mph he was going 70. She flew past like he was stopped. He tried to estimate her speed. As he watched the car disappear around a curve, he thought, That's got to be at least 95. He looked in his mirror to see if the cop was coming too. He wasn't.

John laughed, "He must have written her then and turned back to hide again and—zoom—her car got small!"

As John went around the curve, he saw the Trans-Am nose down in a ditch, about thirty feet off the road. There was steam coming up out of the ditch. The girl was standing nearby. The sleeve on her jump suit was slightly torn, but other than that, she seemed to be OK.

"Are you hurt?" John asked getting out of his car.

"I'm all right, I lost it around that curve, and she headed straight for this watering trough."

John looked at the car. Its nose was down in the ditch in about two feet of water. It looked like the steam was coming from the radiator. It must have hit a rock or something. John noticed other cars stopping. He thought that with other people to help and perhaps the Highway Patrol coming he should get out of there.

He was just waiting for one of the other drivers to get to them so he could wish her luck and drift away, when she asked him if he was going to El Paso. The question surprised him.

"Well, I'm not actually going to El Paso. I'm going through El Paso. I'm taking I-10 all the way to the end, Jacksonville. Why?"

She smiled, "Well, I need to get to Beaumont Texas in time for my daddy's party, and it looks like this beast is going to be out of action for a while." She started taking her small bag out of the trunk of her car as she spoke. "In El Paso I can make arrangements for my car. But since you're going through Beaumont could you please give me a lift there?" She was walking toward him with her bag.

"Am I going through Beaumont?"

"You have to go through Beaumont. It's right on 10."

John thought, I'm out on my own here, I'm driving along, this nice-looking young girl accelerates her car into a ditch in front of me and asks me to give her a lift to Beaumont Texas? And I just happen to be going that way! What the hell.

"OK. But I don't know how big a hurry you're in, I've been on the road all day and I'm planning to stop somewhere up ahead to get some sleep."

"Well," she said handing John her bag, "if you want help, I can drive."

"Yeah, I noticed," he grimaced, "I'll drive."

"I'll just leave a note on the car that I'll send somebody back for it."

John put her bag in the back seat. She held out her hand. "I'm Jennifer Gordon thanks for the help."

"I'm John," he said taking her hand, "let's went. By the way, the first garage I come to or what?"

"I've got Daddy's Texaco card so let's stop at the first one of those we see."

"Oh, this ones on Daddy?" John said realizing he was prying.

"Why suh they're all on Daddy," she replied in a mock southern belle accent only a little thicker than her own. She settled down into the seat as John pulled back on the road.

After driving a couple of miles, John saw a sign that said, "Charleston Carter's Famous Pies just up ahead." John looked at the name again. That's what it said "Charleston Carter." John wondered if there could be more than one Charleston Carter in captivity. After all it's an unusual name. In any event he decided that he was not interested enough in pies to find out if this Charleston Carter was the Charleston Carter he once represented. He must have looked uneasy because Jennifer asked him what was wrong.

"Nothing's wrong," he said. That name is a little unusual that's all." It was a fascinating case and he wanted to tell her about it. "It reminds me of the name of a defendant in a criminal case I covered as a writer on the coast," he lied, making the instant decision that for the all the world, now, he was a crime reporter.

"I met this lawyer named Jack on the coast who was telling me about this case he was working on," he began. And John proceeded to tell her, as though it happened to someone else, about one of his most bazaar cases.

"Charleston Carter was a young Black man with a clean record. He'd come home from culinary college in New Mexico, where he was on an academic scholarship. Charleston had a brother, Jason, who was as bad as Charleston was good, and as dumb as Charleston was bright.

"Part of Jason's problem was that he was tired of hearing their mother always talking about how good her younger son, Charleston, was and how worthless Jason was.

"Charleston always tried to be good to his brother, so when he came home this time, he decided they should spend some time together. Jason asked if they could go for a ride in Charleston's car.

"On the day before Thanksgiving, they went for a ride. Jason said he wanted to get a bottle of fancy bourbon for a birthday present for their mother, whose birthday was the day after Thanksgiving. He asked him to stop outside a liquor store and wait outside while he picked out the present. Charleston was about to tell him that he didn't think their mom would really want him spending his money on liquor, even for her, but he didn't to say anything.

"As Jason entered the store, Charleston waited in the car and was thinking about the inappropriateness of the present Jason wanted to buy. He was annoyed with himself that he didn't try to get Jason to change his mind about buying it. He was having this debate with himself in the car when he heard the shots. Inside the store, Jason had pulled a gun on the owner behind the counter and the owner pulled out his own gun."

John looked to see if she was getting it. "There was an off-duty police man in the store who Jason didn't see as he pulled his gun. A gunfight ensued and the storeowner was killed by either Jason or the cop, and the cop shot and killed Jason. The cop himself was shot in the leg and arm, probably by the storeowner, but was able to get outside and keep Charleston there while the police arrived. The off-duty cop was a hero and Charleston was held as an accomplice in a murder committed in the course of a robbery."

All she said was, "Oh."

"It looked like a real bitch of a case. There was Charleston at the scene with the motor running and his brother inside. Even with his clean record, it didn't look like Charleston was going to convince anyone that he wasn't the look out and get-away driver.

"They went to the preliminary hearing." John explained, "That's to see if there is enough of a case to make a defendant stand trial."

She just nodded.

"The whole story came out just that way. Charleston's attorney didn't see any point in putting Charleston on the stand to tell his 'birthday present story,' because all that was needed to bind Charleston over for trial was a suspicion that a crime was committed and the defendant committed it. On these facts, everyone in the courtroom had a suspicion. The attorney was well aware of the doctrine that mere presence at the scene of the crime is not enough to convict, but he and Charleston both agreed that things looked grim."

"I'll say they looked grim. What happened?"

"Things still looked grim when they went to the arraignment in Superior Court. But when Charleston looked at the judge, something happened. The judge was Carlos Reyes. He was at 34 years old one of the youngest Superior Court judges. Jack thought he was a bright, a good judge, and his getting appointed was helped by being a member of a minority group. He had worked his way up from a pretty poor childhood.

"Anyway, the judge and Charleston each looked at each other as though they had seen each other before but could not remember. Jack could see the puzzlement on both their faces. After the arraignment, Charleston told Jack about his feeling. Jack listened, but all he could say was for Charleston to try and figure out where he knew the judge from. If he did, Jack would have to advise the judge. Maybe the judge needed to disqualify himself, although Jack hoped he wouldn't because he thought he was one of the best judges for giving the defendant an even break. Charleston said he'd think about the judge, he had nothing better to do.

"Three days later, Jack gets a call to see Charleston in jail. After going through the security sally port on the visitor side, Jack could see Charleston waiting with the guard on the inmate side. Charleston was nearly bursting when he started to talk. 'I know where I have seen that man. I know it. I know it.'"

John laughs when he remembers his reaction. "The lawyer says, 'OK. So, tell me. So, tell me.'

"Charleston whispers, 'When I was a kid about fourteen years ago, I was like six. I went with some friends to play basketball. It was on New Year's Day. They took me to a park, way out of our neighborhood. They played a trick on me and left me. I got lost trying to get home. It was dark and I was scared. I didn't know where I was.'

"'So?' The lawyer asks impatiently."

"'So, I was walking near a building that looked like it was being torn down. I was alone and being a kid, I thought I'd get a stick to carry, you know how a six-year-old can get. Well anyway, I went up to this building, and I saw two men arguing. One was old and the other looked like a teenager. I couldn't tell what they were saying because it wasn't in English.

'But anyway, the younger man was screaming at the older. The older man started to reach into his pocket and the younger guy knocked him to the ground. Then he kicked the older man and kicked him again.

'Then the older guy reached for a brick but the young guy grabbed a two-by-four and hit him over the head. He was really mad. He hit him lots of times. Then he realized what he did and started to look around. He didn't see me because I was down in a pile of broken bricks and stuff. He dragged the body a few feet and covered it in a pile of rubble on the other side of the building from where I was.

'As he started to walk away, some broken stucco that my foot was on slipped. I raised up. He looked up and saw me. For a few seconds we just stared at each other. Then I ran. I don't know if he came after me or ran the other way. I didn't turn around to find out—I just got out of there. The man who did the murder was the judge. I swear it,' he said leaning back in his chair."

Jennifer said, "Wow! That's a hell of a story. Are you writing about it? What happened?"

John continued, "Jack told me he just sat there but his mind was racing. He's thinking, What the hell do I do with that! What if he's wrong? Oh shit, what if he's right! Jack could see that Charleston wanted him to say something, but he just had to have time to put this one together. All that came out at first was the cliché. 'Are you sure? It was dark and a long time ago.'

"'I know, I know, I know, but the man knows it was me. I could see that in the courtroom. Man, you never forget shit like that. I can still play that whole scene over in my head. Like it's in slow motion.'

"The lawyer knew: some experiences you can replay for yourself over and over they are that locked into your memory. He needed time to think this one through. He told Charleston he would see him the next day."

"What did he do?" She was getting impatient.

"Well, the lawyer needed to ponder this one long and hard. You just can't walk up to a judge and say, 'Your honor my client thinks he recognizes you from a murder he witnessed fourteen years ago. That would make you around twenty or so judge. Can you tell me what you did New Year's Day that year.' or 'Excuse me judge my client thinks you have a corpse in your closet, how about a break on his case?"

John laughed when he thought about it. "What the hell can the lawyer do? First, he has to find out if Charleston is right? If he's right, does the judge recognize him? If he doesn't, then what? But, if he does—then what does the judge do? How the hell can he disqualify himself? What the hell does he say? He sure as hell isn't going to put it on the record that the killed a guy and this is the witness. The lawyer was stuck. And he knew that it was up to him to come up with the answer."

John saw that she was interested.

"When he went to see Charleston the next day, he tried to pin down the location and the time of the murder.

"Then he talked to his partner who had been a cop. He couldn't tell him why he needed the information but the partner agreed to put the lawyer in touch with one of his old buddies who worked homicides in that area.

"The old homicide detective said they had a report. The old cop remembered the case when John said the building was being torn down and the murder was on New Year's Day. He remembered because of the day, but more so because of the building. Yes, it was being demolished. As it turned out, it was being torn down so they could build the new police station. So, now the lawyer had both the time of the murder and the location.

"The lawyer asks the cop, 'Do you remember if the murderer was ever caught?'

"Cop says, 'I doubt it. We weren't going to look too hard. We knew who the victim was. A real dirtbag. Anybody that had a sister that he turned onto drugs and then put out on the streets could have killed this scumbag and then asked for a medal. I would have given him one. Shit, look for the killer? To buy him a drink maybe.'

"The lawyer thanked the old cop and headed home with his head full of fantasies. Did Carlos Reyes have a sister, or was he just ridding his neighborhood of scum? Was it Reyes at all? Was this really the building site that this Charleston Carter now remembers that six-year-old Charleston Carter being in. Fourteen years is a long time.

"The lawyer still didn't have many of the answers to his questions when the case came up for trial. He did have an idea though. So, now when the judge looked at Charleston, the lawyer thought he saw him trying to place him. Maybe, just maybe. So, just before trial he decides on his strategy. He waives a jury trial."

"What does that mean? Why would he do that?"

"Good question." John, now truly committed to re-living this part of his life in third person narrative, continued "I asked him the same thing myself. He said he might have done it anyway because the judge was a decent judge and the lawyer had learned that if you look at the judge and you would want 12 people just like him on the jury you waive the jury and try the 'mere presence' issue, to the judge. The lawyer had been in the DA's office and knew that if the defense waives jury, even though the prosecution is also entitled to a jury trial, the policy of the DA's office was to waive its right to a jury too. With the waiver of jury, the lawyer also got the prosecutor to put on his case by submitting the transcript of the preliminary hearing. That way the lawyer didn't have to worry about any more evidence than he had already heard."

"I see."

"The lawyer had only Charleston as a witness and his maybe calling his mother for a character witness. The lawyer still wasn't sure of how the information about the judge was useful to him. He had no plan of action in that regard. He knew that on one hand he had this information. On the other hand, he had a good kid with the deck hopelessly stacked against him. If the judge believed Charleston was only there but had no knowledge of his brother's plan, he was home free. If the judge found him not guilty there was not a thing the prosecutor could do about it.

"Now the question was: would the judge let Charleston off the hook forever by the not guilty verdict?

"The lawyer told me that the night before the trial, he had a flash back to when he was a deputy DA. He was in charge of a grand jury investigation into organized crime. He was seeking to get information on some underworld types. He was approached by a lawyer named George who was a good friend of his—they'd gone to college and law school together. George had a problem. He represented a woman who was charged with an assault on her boyfriend in Ventura County. The boyfriend was one of the targets in Jack's investigation. George, had tried to get his lady off the hook up in Ventura by offering the DA up there her information on the boyfriend's activity in exchange for a pass on the assault. No deal. Now, George had a simple proposition. He would have our guy, Jack, the friendly DA, call her as a witness before the grand jury. As a witness she would be given immunity from prosecution for any transaction she testified to. George promised Jack she would be a willing witness. All he wanted in exchange was for Jack 'to stumble into the assault a little bit' while asking about her connection with these people. That way he could go up to Ventura and tell the DA to stick it in his ass—she had immunity.

"So, Jack thought about the proposition. He couldn't understand the Ventura DA's priorities. He checked and found out George was telling the truth. Except for the assault charge, which she might even beat on a 'self-defense' issue, she only had prior conviction for trespassing, which had been knocked down from a soliciting for purposes of prostitution charge five years earlier when she would have been around 19."

Jennifer asked, "How's that again?" By knocked down do you mean she was charged with prostitution and gets convicted of trespassing?"

"Yep. In those cases, the DA wants to clear the calendar and offers the trespass as a plea deal. Which the girls jump at because, if you get convicted of prostitution a second time it is mandatory jail time. So, one way you avoid the second offense is not getting the first one." John laughed, "Sometimes I overheard lawyers trying to explain to their client why they were in effect pleading guilty to trespassing in their own bedroom."

When Jennifer laughed, John continued, "So the lawyer told me he thought about it and wondered why the Ventura DA up there didn't buy the deal for her testimony. He knew there would be some flack if he wiped out the Ventura case without talking to them, but he also knew that he could easily widen one or two of his questions so that he would be asking questions to which her answer would be responsive and would let him get some more helpful information for himself and it would also let George's client skate. So, Jack called up to Ventura. The deputy that got on the phone gave him the 'Well, what are you boys in the big city up to now?' routine. Before Jack hung up his decision was made. He decided he didn't like that stuffed shirt up there anyway. When he called the woman to the witness stand before the grand jury, he had no problem getting her to tell him about her boyfriend and how she came to assault him. The DA in Ventura was just out of luck.

"OK. So now Charleston's trial started with the submission on the transcript. Then the lawyer, deciding not to call the mother, called Charleston to the stand. Charleston told his story. He admitted his brother had problems. But he would not jeopardize all he worked for to help him rob a store. He most assuredly did not know his brother had intended to rob the store and he certainly did not know his brother had a gun.

"It was on cross examination that it happened. The prosecutor was having Charleston go over his testimony once more looking for a flaw or an inconsistency to dive into. He asked, in a tone dripping in sarcasm, 'And you want this court to believe that you would not do such a thing?'

"Charleston turned and looked right at the judge. 'Your honor, I grew up in a bad neighborhood. I am trying to work my way up out of that neighborhood through college. I would not be involved with anything like this. I have seen some terrible things happen in my life. When I was six years old, I saw a man murdered, beaten to death with a two-by-four on New Year's Day. It was in a building that was being torn down to make way for the police station. And that memory still stays in my mind.'

"Charleston was talking so softly that the judge had been leaning forward a little just to hear the testimony. Jack couldn't help but look up at the judge. It seemed, as though the judge was looking at Charleston and still trying to figure out where he had seen him before, when the impact of Charleston soft words exploded up at him.

"The judge leaned motionless for a second and then allowed himself to settle back in his seat while looking to see if anyone in the court room could see his reaction.

"In the middle of the cross examination, Judge Reyes called for a recess. It took the prosecutor by surprise. He wasn't watching the judge as closely as Jack had been. In fact, so sure was he of his case that he seemed to be going through the motions of a cross-examination and hardly listening to Charleston's testimony at all.

"Jack was wondering what the hell he was going to say if the judge called them into chambers. He didn't. Within minutes, Reyes was back on the bench. He was composed. The prosecutor finished the cross-examination and the case was submitted.

"The judge asked for brief argument. The prosecutor outlined the evidence and then asked for a conviction.

"Jack was unaware of exactly what he was going to say until he stood up. 'Your Honor, the issue here is whether you believe my client that he was merely at the scene and knew nothing of his brothers plans. The evidence is clear that he was at the scene and we do not deny it. My client is a good student and he is trying to raise himself out of the poverty of his childhood through education. He has testified, and I would not raise the issue other than as comment on the testimony, that he was once at the scene of another crime as a child and that made a great impression on him. It is unfortunate that he was at the scene of his brother's crime. But, I submit, your honor, that my client is no more guilty of this crime than he was of the crime he witnessed when he was six-year-old.'"

Jennifer screamed, "Brilliant! Sounds like the kind of lawyer I'd want if I ever needed one."

John just smiled, "After the prosecutor took his last shot at convincing the judge, Jack and Charleston rose at the counsel table to hear the judge's decision. The judge looked down from the bench and said, 'I am aware of the admonition that says 'Judge not lest ye be judged,' but I am a judge and I must judge. Very often the children of God, and we are all God's children, find themselves in strange circumstances. Circumstances that are not of their making. Circumstances they would change if they could, but they are powerless to change. I think Mr. Carter, you have found yourself in situations which were not of your making. And I note with sadness that you lost a brother.

"'Perhaps, he was lost because of his own problems, but he is lost to you none the less. I too, once lost a brother out of his own problems. Certainly, there were others who fed his problems and lived off them, but they were his problems none the less. His loss is with me still.

"He caught Jack's sympathetic glance.

"'More to the point, I note that the rule in cases where the evidence is purely circumstantial, is that the evidence of guilt must not only be proof guilt beyond a reasonable doubt but must also be inconsistent with innocence. Since I do believe that this situation was, in fact, not of your own making, just like the one you witnessed as a young child, I find you not guilty.'

"Judge Reyes looked at Jack and their eyes met. The lawyer nodded a silent assurance that as far as he was concerned the case was closed. Judge Reyes nodded slowly that he understood and slowly returned to his chambers."

"Wow! That's a hell of a story are you writing about that?"

John smiled, "No not yet."

He thought about Charleston Carter. He wondered if he really had to anything to do with famous pies. He knew as he drove with Jennifer that he could not find out today. He knew in fact that he could not risk finding out this day or any day. That thought started to make him sad.

Jennifer asked, "What happened to the judge?"

"I don't know," said John. "I never asked the lawyer, and he never told me."

When they got into El Paso, John said, "Let's find a Texaco station and take care of that business and get off the road. I'm beat." He found a station.

John stayed in the car while Jennifer went inside. She had told him that she was going to call "Daddy" and have him speak to the garage man about the arrangements for the car. John started to get the feeling that "Daddy" was a powerful land baron who could reach out and take care of his "little girl" wherever she might be.

When Jennifer got back to the car, John asked if she knew the town well enough to recommend a place to spend the night.

"That depends on whether we want one room or two," she replied.

John was thinking about doing a "What kind of a guy do you think I am" routine but he was too tired. John heard himself saying "Look we've known each other for almost a whole two hours. It's up to you."

"Then I'll take care of it," she said, and gave him directions to a motel without any indication of which choice she'd made.

When they got to the motel, Jennifer stopped John from getting out. "I said I'd take care of it," she said and walked into the office to register. As she was coming out John tried to see if she had only key or two but couldn't tell. He was not going to ask. His motto had long been, "If it's good news it can wait and if it's bad news, you'll hear about it soon enough."

Jennifer told him to drive around the back of the building to the right and park. She was watching John for a reaction. When the car stopped, she turned around on her knees in the front seat to get her bag out of the back. She tried to sound off hand as she said "Oh, you're in room 242." She pulled her bag out of the back seat and stood outside the car. She looked at the key in her hand, and I'm in room 2—4—2. We hope y'all find that satisfactory," she added in her put-on drawl.

As tired as he was, John still felt a surge of excitement at the thought of maybe lying next to the body under that jumpsuit. He knew that Jennifer was still looking for a reaction from him, now maybe more than before. She had put herself on the line, so to speak. Now, if he kept up the pokerfaced show of indifference she might be hurt. John reached out and put an arm around her shoulder and gave a squeeze. As soon as his arm went around her shoulder, John realized he had a problem with the money.

John had kept the money locked in the trunk of the car, hidden under the spare tire while he was in the car. Except for his brief trips to the men's room at rest stops, the car had not been out of his sight. When he was at the motel, the other night the money was in the bed with him. John was now worried that if he left the money in the car, this girl who he hardly knew might awaken in the night and take the car and keep going to her "Daddy" with it. On the other hand, if he took the money into the room, how could he get it there without her seeing, and where could he hide it there. He certainly couldn't keep in on him.

He let his arm slip from her shoulder and let her go up ahead of him. He explained he wanted to check to see if the car was locked. Jennifer was already on the outside steps that led up to the room when John decided what he would do. He would leave the money in the trunk, but he opened the hood and took off the wire that runs from the ignition coil to the distributor so that the car wouldn't start. John had actually learned that trick from one of his cases in the DA's office. He was the prosecutor of a man charged with rape. This man's method of operation was to find a woman who had gone by herself to a concert like at the Greek Theater or the Santa Monica Civic.

During the concert, he would sneak out and undo the wire just as John had. This disabled his prospective victim's car. When the concert was over and everybody was leaving for home, he would offer to stay with the stranded woman and when the time was right, he'd make his move. John put the wire in the trunk, near the money the wire's presence in its new location was designed to protect, then he went up to the room.

When John got to the room, Jennifer was scanning through TV channel guide. John was exhausted. There were two beds in the room so he put his stuff on the one closest to the door. Jennifer was already seated at the foot of the other one fiddling with one of the channels. He looked at the car parked outside. He was glad he could see it from the window. He started to unpack the stuff he had just bought. He wondered if Jennifer would notice everything was new. Maybe she would think he had class. He looked at her. She now had her shoes off and was sitting Indian style on the end of the bed watching the news.

John thought about the situation. He thought he was expected to make some kind of move. He was excited by looking at her and knowing they were alone together but he felt awkward now. He wanted to take a shower. He decided he'd shower and then see what he felt like afterward. John tucked the keys to the car into his toiletry bag, stripped to his underwear and strode between Jennifer and the TV set.

He liked hotel showers. They seemed to have much better water pressure or something. He was wondering if she was going to "surprise" him by joining him.

He was disappointed that she didn't. When he got out of the bathroom, the TV was still going but she was asleep. The jumpsuit was on the chair near her head. He saw her light brown hair covering the pillow. He wondered if she was wearing anything under the sheet. He also studied her for a while trying to decide if she was really sleeping. He shrugged, turned off the TV, and went to sleep.

In the morning, he woke up to the sound of Jennifer coming out of the bathroom wrapped in a towel saying, "Well, it's comforting to know I'm rooming with an honorable man."

Then she sat on the edge of her bed closest to his bed as she was drying her hair.

She asked, "How far do you think we will get today?"

"I don't know," he smiled, "What are we talking about?"

She laughed when she realized what she'd said.

"I guess a girl has to watch what she says around you."

"Well, a girl who looks as good as you does."

"Oh, so you like the way I look. I didn't think you noticed."

"Gosh, Did I seem cold? Miss Jennifer. Well, it's only 'cause my Mammy done tol' me to bewar of strangers.'"

She laughed, moved over and sat on his bed putting her hand on his knee. "What else did Mammy tell you about?"

John dropped the accent, "I think now we are getting into the area that my father told me about."

She stood up and dropped the towels to the floor. She watched John's reaction to seeing her body before she slid under the sheets with him.

John reached to hug her and she put her arms around him. The force of her hug startled him. She was starting to kiss him and the kisses were hard. Her hug, forceful before, started to increase in intensity.

She rolled on top of him in such a swift smooth motion that John was surprised by it. He was truly puzzled by the passion she was showing.

All of a sudden, he realized that she was starting without him. He thought that he had better get his mind on what he was doing or she was going to finish without him too.

Then she began filling John's mouth with her tongue as she reached down for him again making sure he was good and hard. She got to her knees and straddled his legs She lowered herself down on him in this position. She started using her legs to make herself go up and down on him. "My sister told me about this position. They call it 'Cowgirl' what do you think? Is it OK for you?"

John had never been asked that question before. He stopped to think about it. He like the sensations he was feeling.

"I love it," he said.

He looked up and saw her eyes were closed tightly. He put his hands on her breasts as they hung above his face. As he started to rub her nipples slowly, he closed his eyes and saw the prostitute in the gold lame mini dress walking toward the streets just as she had in the bar.

In his mind he was with her on the street. It was her he was in bed with. It was her breasts in his hands. John felt a pain in his legs. Jennifer had wrapped her legs around his legs in such a way that her feet came around his legs and rested on his shins. As she pushed her pelvis against his with all her force, the bones in her ankles and feet hurt his shins. The pain brought him out of his fantasy.

He wanted to be good. He tried to match her intensity. Yet, at times he seemed to be outside himself watching his performance. When he tried to concentrate on his own pleasure, he was distracted by the tightness of her grasp on him, her pulling him toward her, the rolling of her hips and her screams. Her first orgasm surprised him. He didn't realize that she was that far along. He was also surprised when he realized that her first orgasm was not also going to be her last.

This was new, different. He stopped trying to get pleasure himself and just tried to give. He found himself repeating things that Marsha enjoyed—but they had no effect on Jennifer. Yet, the way she behaved it seemed to him that he must be doing something right. She started to scream again. It frightened him at first. He was worried that she was making so much noise that someone might call the police. When her screaming subsided, he thought he could try for his own pleasure now, but was distracted when his movement started her off again. After her screams subsided this time, she looked down at John and smiled. He recalled the image of the girl in the bar.

With this orgasm he could feel as she tightened around him. After a few minutes she got off, turned around and came down facing him. He pulled her over so he could kiss her and his hands instinctively went for her breasts. He again checked out the warm wet sensations he was getting from being back inside her.

"I think I like this position better," he said."

"Me too," she laughed and kissed him more deeply.

He watched her face and she was about to reach orgasm again. Then just as she was about to let go, she hugged him tighter as if she was trying to pull his whole body inside hers. She let out a gasp and let go. She kept moving her hips and he watched her face.

She put his hands to her breast. She asked, "Squeeze me?"

John rubbed her nipples between his thumbs and fore-finger.

"Harder," she said

John squeezed harder. She seemed to get more and more excited. "Harder" she said again.

John didn't think he could squeeze any harder. He was starting to feel that he was squeezing much too hard already. He thought that if he had squeezed Marsha the way that was squeezing Jennifer, in response to her first request, Marsha would have gotten out of bed and hit him with something. But this was not Marsha. No matter how much pressure he put on Jennifer's nipples she wanted more.

He could feel that she was coming again. This time much stronger that the first. As she came, she collapsed on John's chest. Then she sat up and rubbed her nipples with her hands. John could see her smile. She got off him and cuddled under his arm. She took him in her hand and started to kiss him around his face. Then around his neck and down his chest. She looked at him and smiled. There was no question in John's mind where she was heading. When she arrived John thought "No. This definitely is not Marsha."

He felt her hand grab him. He liked what she was doing with her mouth but her hand was griping him too tightly. He reached down to loosen her fingers.

"Too tight?"

The question embarrassed John.

"A little," he said.

"How's this," she asked.

John checked it for a few strokes.

"Much better," he said.

"Good!"

John lay back and tried to concentrate on the sensations.

He could feel that his leg muscles and back muscles were like burning knots that were starting to slowly loosen. He could feel that he was still in her mouth

He came soon after. When he had finished, John opened his eyes and was surprised to see a face other than Marsha's.

He was starting to get soft. Her tongue licking the tip of his penis started to be an irritating feeling. She could sense this and she stopped. She lay down beside him again. He was starting to breathe more slowly now. She could feel his heart pounding as she put her head on his chest.

He felt drained. He just lay there running his hand down her arm. He ran his hands to her nipples assure himself that they were all right. She knew what he was doing.

"I like it like that," she said. "When I get started, I don't like it too hard. But when I'm warmed up, the harder the better."

"But isn't it painful?"

"Well, it's a pleasure-pain."

John had never heard that before.

She looked at the clock radio and it was after 10 a.m. She gave John a kiss on the cheek.

"Are you OK?" she asked.

"I'm fine," he smiled.

He rolled to the side of the bed with one arm still under her. He wondered how anybody could call two sex organs going at each other to achieve their own gratification "making love."

She put her ear on his chest and played with the hair. He wanted to ask how he had done but couldn't. Besides he knew it was a stupid question. He had no doubt that she had a good time. He was just not sure how much of it was due to him.

He felt both elated and empty. It wasn't great, after all she was a woman he had just met. He'd have to get to know her better, not be distracted by her movements, to experience real pleasure with her. But it wasn't, "What-did-I-do-that-for?"

It was just that the anticipation was a whole lot better than the reality. He thought, So, what else is new? But he was still puzzled by her intensity and passion. It didn't seem to fit.

Now, lying there with her she was still holding him tightly. He read it as affection and was suspicious of how he could be the object of that amount of affection so quickly. There was no question that by any standards she was a beautiful woman, one any man would want to have. But what the hell did she see in him? They stayed in bed and talked for a while about themselves. John, even with his newly created crime-reporter persona, was still being very careful about what he revealed. At one point, he wondered what if anything she was hiding. After all, if he was speaking with "forked tongue" about some things so could she. But his part was made quite a bit easier by the fact that she seemed to want to tell him everything about herself and "Daddy."

"Daddy" was pretty much as John had suspected. She also revealed that she told "Daddy" that she was getting a lift all the way home. And "Daddy" insisted that John was invited to the party that he was giving. It was an annual affair. In fact, it was "Daddy's" birthday party. He gave himself a lavish barbecue birthday bash each year.

"Everybody comes to Daddy's parties."

John wondered what "Daddy's" reaction would be if he saw them right now. He suspected that his would be the first case on record were a man died twice in two separate states within the space of a week.

They got up and got dressed.

He suggested they get some breakfast at the motel restaurant before getting on the road.

She said, "If you like Mexican food, we can pop over the border to Juarez. There's a great place I know there and we can also get gas at about one third the price."

She seemed pleased with her idea.

He was on the spot. There was no way he wanted to get near that border. He didn't want to be put in any situation where he would have to identify himself.

It was just a precaution. But he believed in taking precautions.

"Look, Jen, we're here and the restaurant is here. I don't see why I have to leave my homeland, land of my birth," he saluted, "to get a couple of eggs and cheap gas."

"I'm sorry," she laughed, "I didn't realize I was dealing with such a patriot."

He replied, "Buy American!"

They ate at the hotel and he was pleased that he had gotten off the hook.

El Paso to Beaumont took three driving days. John had not realized just how big Texas was. They drove through the night and caught a couple of winks at a rest stop one night. When they stopped for the night in a hotel the next night, Jennifer, again, insisted on paying for the room. John never asked her how she registered them.

He thought to himself that they might have sex in the morning as they had the time before. When they got up to the room, they both went to sleep. But the next morning when she woke him, she was dressed and packed.

John was disappointed but he tried not to show it. He still kept the distributor wire in the trunk, he had decided that it was a wise precaution whenever he left the car for any length of time.

So, he went out to the car with his own bag and "checked under the hood."

When they arrived at Jennifer's home it was dark. John let her drive the last few miles. The house was large but not ornate. It was not Bel Aire but it was bigger and comfortable. John thought that "big and comfortable" would be a good description for "Daddy."

He was so effusive in his thanks for John having taken care of his "little girl" that when John got over the fact that he really did refer to Jennifer as "My little girl," he started feeling guilty about having slept with her.

John's few things were put in the guest room, which was on the other side of the house from where the family's rooms were. John was wondering if he was going to get to play with Jennifer again. He doubted it. He started to feel put out.

The house was buzzing with party preparations. The big deal was the next day. John really had no plans for when he was going to get back on the road. That in a way was a unique feeling. He could do whatever he wanted. He thought for a moment of what was going on back home. He wondered about Marsha but then got caught up envisioning the daily life that was going on without him. Cars were filling the freeway. Lawyers were walking into the courthouse. All the stuff he would be looking at if he were home was going on—it was just that he was not a part of it.

The next morning the house was full of people getting ready for other people. John felt alone in this milling of strangers. He went out and looked at the grounds. He had not gotten a good look at them the night before. The place was huge. John could hardly believe the pool. It was so big it actually had islands in it. They were about five feet in diameter. John wondered if they were supposed to be lily pads or something.

The guests started arriving at about 11 a.m. The huge grounds around the house were filling with people. John walked outside. There were tables everywhere. He hadn't seen them the night before. He didn't know if they had just appeared or he had missed them. He saw a large grill area with eight or ten men in aprons putting on all sorts of meats and chicken. There was a bar that was set up with four bartenders behind it. There was already a crowd around it. He looked at his watch it was 11:45. He shook his head. He had never seen anything like it. The people kept arriving. They were walking down the long road from the gate. The fence on both side of the gate was screened by trees so John couldn't see exactly how the people were arriving but from the crowd it looked like some were coming by bus.

While he was studying the situation, Jennifer came up behind him and took his arm. She was wearing an off the shoulder party dress.

"How did you sleep?"

"Alone." He looked around.

"Have you had breakfast yet?"

"Nope, I might as well wait and make it lunch. That stuff on the grill looks pretty good. Quite a group you've got here."

"Nobody misses one of Daddy's parties. I have to play hostess. I'll see you later." She rushed off to join her father and a rather distinguished looking gentleman.

John stood by a tree and watched her go.

"That's Willard Pless," said a voice from behind him. He turned around and saw a stunningly beautiful woman with shoulder length blond hair. She was really breathtaking.

John just looked and thought, State of the Art.

She took another sip from her almost empty glass and continued. "He is an Associate Justice of the Texas Supreme Court." Jennifer is going to be nice to him so he will let her fiancé be his law clerk get when he finishes school."

She eyed John up and down, and said, "You look like the last man to sleep with Jennifer."

John's eyes widened, "Excuse me, but don't you have to read me my rights or something before you charge me with doing things like that. I mean I watch TV I know how that's done."

He was talking to stall for time. He didn't have any idea what was going on and he didn't like it.

"I'm Gerry Gordon. Jennifer's cousin," she didn't look up. Her piercing blue eyes just studied the bottom of her now empty glass.

"Well, I guess you know who I am. That's a hell of an approach you've got there. Do you get many men to confess?"

"No need for a confession. You're a man. You've spent more than a day with Jennifer. You've slept with her.

"All you need to do to sleep with Jennifer once is to be a man. She uses sex as some kind of sorting out process. If she likes you in bed you can be her friend for life. But, don't count on ever sleeping with her again."

John was a bit hurt and a bit angry. He wondered if what she said was true. Looking at his watch he asked, "How long does it take for a guy to sleep with you?"

"You're married," she said knowingly.

"Well, I was married," he paused, "but one of us died."

She wasn't even slowed down by the thought that he might actually be a widower.

No false, "Oh I'm so sorry." She just blasted straight ahead.

"You look married," she nodded, "and I never sleep with a married man, not even my husband."

She started to walk away. "And, besides, I was always told, ever since I could listen, that I could never take things from Cousin Jennifer."

As she walked away, John wasn't sure what had just happened to him or why. He looked for Jennifer and saw her in an animated conversation with a young man while she was wrapping the judge's arm around her waist.

John wondered if the young man was the fiancé Jennifer never mentioned. He wondered if the fiancé was the only man to sleep with her more than once.

John saw the scene from the outside looking in. He didn't know if he felt hurt or foolish. He didn't feel that he wanted to hang around and try to become a part of the crowd he saw at the party. It just seemed like a bigger version of some of the Hollywood parties Marsha would drag him to whenever any of her "friends" from her health studio or wherever invited them.

He didn't need to be Jennifer's friend for life. He knew it was time to say goodbye, if he could get the word in, and get back on the road.

NINE

While John was approaching New Orleans, he decided it was time to stop and lay over a couple of days. He realized that even though for the first time in as long as he could remember he had no time limits, he was still pushing himself. He was driving constantly. He missed looking around Houston and San Antonio because he was in a hurry to get Jennifer to Beaumont. Now, he decided he was going to get off the road and stay at least two nights.

John found a hotel and registered. He parked the car in their lot and disabled it, but stuffed the money in his bag. He took the elevator to his room. He wasn't sure what he wanted to do with the rest of the night. He decided to take a shower., then get dressed to go down to the restaurant in the hotel. When he got to the lobby, he thought he would take a walk around the French Quarter rather than stay in the hotel to eat.

It was dark by now and there was music coming from somewhere down the street. He headed toward it.

The place was dimly lit and the band was just taking a break. John ordered a beer and took it to a corner booth. He sat by himself and watched the people. He thought, OK, so this is New Orleans.

A waitress came over and smiled. John ordered another beer. The second beer was making him pleasantly light headed. He felt like being that way. He just wanted to turn sideways and stretch his legs out on the seat and watch the parade of people. He closed his eyes for a while and let the tension of driving flow out of him. He felt it was the first time he had relaxed, really relaxed since he got on the road. He thought that in the morning he would be a tourist.

"What can I do touristy?" he asked when his third beer arrived. He answered his own question before she could. "I know I'll take a sightseeing bus."

She helped, "Well they leave from in front the hotel up the block. There's an ad for them in the hotel lobby."

He was pleased with his plan. After a while, he got up and decided to head back to the hotel. He walked back up the block, but just when he could see his hotel, he decided to turn around and go in the other direction thinking he would circumnavigate the block, just to see what was there.

He walked down Bourbon Street. There was a crowd milling around. Many of them had oversized paper cups full of beer or frozen drinks. John saw a corner stand and sneered at the inflated prices of the oversized drinks. Then he bought one.

He noticed that everyone was looking at a young woman in a low-cut formal dress who was on an ornate, wrought iron balcony. From the white tuxedos of the two men and the matching dress of another woman further back on the balcony, John assumed they were from a wedding party. The woman who had the crowd's attention had one of the oversized cups in her hand and she leaned over the balcony talking to some of the sailors in the crowd below. As she leaned down her nipples came over the top of her gown. The crowd cheered. She stood up and the crowd booed. She tossed some ice from her drink down to the sailors. Then she leaned over the rail to catch it as they threw it back. The crowd cheered. She stood up and they booed. But this time when they booed, she pulled a strap from the dress off her shoulder and showed a breast while she gyrated her hips.

A sailor started to climb one of the poles that supported the balcony. She saw him and ran to the other end. At first, she seemed frightened by the climber, but when she saw he was handing a cup with a drink to one of the tuxedoed young men up there with her, she laughed and started her little show further down the balcony.

John watched the performance of the woman and the crowd for a few minutes. He felt isolated. He told himself he should lighten up and enjoy the night, but he found it hard to let go. He wandered away from the crowd.

Walking aimlessly for a few blocks, he saw a park across the street. The park had a big statue of Louis Armstrong. He took a brief walk around. He thought of the man and his music. He headed back to his hotel.

In the hotel lobby, he saw the glass door to the marquee board opened. He watched the old white-haired Black man as he worked and thought how distinguished he looked. Then he saw what the plastic white letters that the old man was sticking on the board said, "Welcome National District Attorney's Association. Reception in the Cajun Ro. . ." John assumed that the rest of the sentence was going to specify the Cajun Room and a time, but he didn't really want to stay any longer to find out. He asked at the desk.

"Yes," the district attorneys convention was starting tomorrow evening some of the guests had already checked in. John told the man he wouldn't be able to stay the next night after all.

As John took the elevator up to his room he thought, What are the odds on that. Oh well, so much for being touristy. Tomorrow morning, we get on the road again.

John knew first hand that the fact that he was far away from home didn't preclude the kind of chance encounter he wanted to avoid. Once, John had had to go to San Diego to handle an arraignment. He originally thought it would be a good one-day vacation for himself.

When the arraignment was done, he thought he would go over to the Embarcadero area to get an early lunch before heading north for home. He was sitting in the restaurant for a while when he saw Bob Martin come in with a woman. Bob Martin had been a deputy DA when John had joined the office, and he had left shortly after that to become a judge in the Beverly Hills Municipal court. He and Bob where not close, but John knew him well enough to know that the attentive young lady holding hands with "His honor" was not his wife.

John felt a little uneasy sitting at his table as Bob and this woman walked by. John had been a criminal defense lawyer long enough know the importance of looking the other way. He pretended he was invisible. Bob hadn't seemed to notice him and that made things a bit easier. John thought he might leave the restaurant but the waitress was just bringing his order. Shortly after the waitress took their order the woman with Bob headed for the lady's room. John was surprised when Bob came over and sat down. John didn't know how to address him, certainly "Judge" or "Your Honor" might seem a little sarcastic under the circumstances. He opted for "Hi, Bob."

Bob gave him a shrug, "What can I say? This is damn awkward."

"Look Bob, it might be awkward if I was here—but I'm not. This is none of my business. I figure to eat and leave. As far as I'm concerned neither of us is here."

But it was obvious that Bob needed to talk about it—to make it seem like it was all right.

"She's the office manager for one of the doctors in Beverly Hills. She appeared before me in Small Claims matters a few times." As a nervous after thought he added, "I guess I'll have to disqualify myself from now on. Oh, shit how is that going to look! God. How do I explain that?" he turned to John.

John just sat. Before he could answer the rhetorical question, he was handed a more personal one. "John, how long have you been married?"

John knew what was coming next so he got right to the point. "Look, Bob, the closest I've come to being with another woman was when I represented a couple of Hell's Angels on a matter in Norwalk and they wanted to give me one of their women because they liked the job I did for them. Marsha was away for that week and I thought about the offer but turned it down. It seemed like a real cold thing—too cold for me. Besides I felt like it might be some sort of set up."

He turned to Bob, "Look, I already said this is none of my business, Bob, I'm not here, let's just leave it at that OK?"

When the girlfriend returned Bob stood up but did not introduce her. They just walked together back to their table. When John was finished, he nodded to Bob as he left. He realized that Bob should probably disqualify himself if he appeared before him too, but he thought they could cross that bridge if and when they came to it. As John remembered the incident now, he was pleased that he never had to appear before Bob Martin again.

In the morning, John paid his hotel bill. Got his deposit, and refund for the night not stayed, and headed out wondering if anybody from LA who could recognize him who was going to be at the conference. No matter, he was more interested in getting on the road.

Once he was back on I-10, he thought about his situation and his options. He thought if he had run into anyone, he could say that his disappearance was a hush hush thing arraigned by the Feds. Or, he could say that when he found out that Snappy got shot, he felt that they would be looking for him so he decided to drop out of sight. He thought, OK so why didn't you tell someone you could trust that you were going, he asked himself. Well, who the hell can you trust? Anybody who is big enough to take out Snappy McNeal has got to have a lot of juice.

As he drove and carried on the debate with himself, he started to wonder who had killed Snappy and whether he really was in some danger. He thought the hit could have come from Snappy's organization—from the other members of the group known on the street as the Magnificent Seven or just the Mag 7.

He wondered if the hit could have come from above "the 7" or below it. He assumed that whoever did it was afraid that if the pressure was applied really hard, Snappy might just give someone up to save his own ass.

He thought about Snappy. He tried to sift through all he knew about him to try to come up with some answers. He made a list of possible enemies. He labeled his mental list, Benefactors of Death.

John had been working alone late one night at his office on Hollywood Boulevard. He was in the back room that served as a combination law library and conference room when he heard the door to the office waiting room open. He expected it to be the cleaning woman. He waited a minute to hear the sound of the vacuum cleaner. When he heard the door open a second time, he went to check it out. In the waiting room area were two men. One was light-skinned Black who looked to be in his late twenties. His three-piece suit neatly covered the big man and showed his broad chest and shoulders. His companion was a huge Black man with long corn rowed hair and weight lifter arms. His upper body was bulging out of a gold sequined tank top. The bodyguard-type was making a great display of his looking the wood paneled room over as though he was so bad he'd be ready if the walls tried to attack him or the man he was obviously there to protect.

John was not impressed. He had seen the show before.

"You guys look too well dressed to be burglars," John said, as he started to put down the book he had brought out of his library.

It was then that Billy Cooks introduced himself and said he needed to talk. John was about to tell him to come back during normal business hours, but he decided he didn't have the energy to play the scene too hard. Besides, he felt he needed a break from the research he was doing. He walked into his office and made a motion for Cooks to follow him. The bodyguard started to come too. John spoke to the power. "I guess it is fair to say you came to see me in my capacity as an attorney at law."

Cooks just nodded.

"Whatever you and I say is to each other when I act in that capacity is usually a privileged communication. That means under normal circumstances I can't tell any-one even a judge what you and I talked about. But if there is a third party present it usually vitiates—that is wipes out—the privilege."

Cooks turned to his man and said softly, "I'll be all right."

John looked at Cooks, who looked big enough so that he could be somebody else's bodyguard, and realized that the assumption Cooks had made—that he'd be safe being alone with John—was a good one.

When they were alone in the room, John sat on the couch rather than behind his desk. Cooks sat in the chair that was in front of the desk, between the desk and the couch.

"Mr. Cooks, what can I do for you," John started out.

"I have a girl friend who's in jail because of me and I would like you to get her out. I'll pay the bills but I don't want people to know I'm involved."

"If this lady agrees to have me act as her lawyer, and if I agree to take the case, my concern will then be for her best interests no matter who pays the bills. As long as you understand that, I see no problems. Where is she now and what's her name?

"Betina Swift and she's in SBI."

"Why?"

"They say they found a gun on the back seat of her car."

"Did they?"

"Yeah, I guess they did."

"You say she's in jail because of you. How's that."

"The cops been watchin' one of the apartment buildings I own. I go there on occasion. They're putting the heat on pretty good to see if I make a mistake. They're trying to catch me meeting with certain people. They say I'm involved in drugs."

John just looked. He was not going to ask the obvious, "Are you?" Instead, he asked what he really needed to know. "How'd Betina Swift get popped because of that?"

"She and I had a date last night and she was supposed to pick me up at my place. Then I got a call to sit still. You know—don't go nowhere, I might need you later.' After the call, I forgot about her coming by. When she knocked on my door, I told her about the situation, and she left right away. When she was getting back in the car, a guy in a suit came up to her and started to talk to her and then a police car pulled up and the cop from the police car opened the door to her car and found the gun. I saw the whole thing from my window. They took her away. I'd like you to get the bail thing taken care of for me and handle the case."

John quoted a fee and was not surprised when Cooks stepped outside the door and after a few seconds came back with the cash. John agreed to see Betina Swift in the morning at Sibyl Brand Institute. He told Cooks that he would hold the money until he could find out if she wanted him to represent her. He was curious how Cooks had decided on him, but he did not ask.

The next afternoon John was sitting across the interview room partition from a very attractive Betina Swift. She agreed that she wanted John to represent her. She had heard of him from someone where she worked but they didn't get into who or where she worked. She described the events leading to her arrest the same way Cooks had—except she added one detail.

She said, "Cooks told me he was waiting for a call from his boss, Snappy McNeal. When the cop stopped me in the street, he had asked me how I know Cooks and McNeal." It was the first time John had heard the name Snappy McNeal other than in rumors. Betina said the car and the gun belonged to her brother. She didn't know the gun was in the back seat when she borrowed the car.

It looked to John that she was just stopped because the detective thought she might have information on Cooks or McNeal. She confirmed that when she said the detective as much as told her so when he visited her at SBI that morning. "I told the detective I already gave him everything I knew about Cooks—I only went out with the man twice before. I don't know nothing about his business or who he does business with. All the cop did was shrug and said I was 'collateral damage' and should pick my boy friends more carefully."

John told her the case might not go past the preliminary hearing. "This detective knows he had no probable cause to stop you. If he knows you are no further use to him, he may not even bother to show up to testalie at the prelim." John noted she did not seem to be surprised by his use of the word. If they need the detective and the cop from the black and white and only the cop shows up, if we have any kinda decent judge you should walk. I had one of these a while back."

When John left the interview room, he called a bail bondsman and made arrangements for Betina's released.

As John suspected, the case never got past the preliminary hearing. The courtroom was empty when John and Betina arrived. In the hall, John saw one young man who looked like a police officer with a large envelope that John assumed contained the gun. John kept waiting as the time for the hearing was approaching but no one who looked like he could be a detective appeared. As the case was called, John thought, It's Reggie-Johnson-time. The old they-need-two cops-but-they-only-got-one trick. He leaned over to Betina and whispered, "Just sit tight I don't think this will take too long."

John sat back as the young Deputy DA led the officer through his testimony about being on patrol the night in question; receiving a call to assist a detective at the address in question; opening the door to read the vehicle identification number on the door post; seeing the gun in plain sight on the back seat sticking out from under a male's sport jacket; seizing the gun, and placing the defendant under arrest.

When the officer was finished, John stood up and said he had no questions.

The DA smiled—thinking he had left no loose ends for John to pick at— and asked that the gun be admitted into evidence.

John objected. "Your Honor, the people have failed to show any probable cause for detaining my client in the first instance." He sat down.

As expected, the DA asked for time to call the detective, but the judge was having none of it. The judge looked over to John who stood up and was closing his file.

The judge looked down at the deputy DA, and shook his head. "I'm sorry counsel but this case is dismissed. Next time, if you are not ready, don't answer that you are."

John stayed on his feet and turned to Betina. She was shaking her head and smiling. "So cold, my man is so cold."

John smiled, "Just don't ask me to get the gun back. Also, if they really want you on this one, they may re-file but from what you tell me…"

"That's OK, whatever they do, they do. Don't worry about the gun, my brother has another one. He says that in his line of work he'd rather be caught with it than without it."

John resisted asking about her brother's line of work, but he assumed that he worked with Billy Cooks who worked for a man named Snappy McNeal.

John and Betina had stayed in touch as he called to thank her each time he was retained by a new client she referred.

It wasn't long before the police got a tip and played it into the break they were looking for. They raided the apartment claiming it was a Mag 7 stash house for drugs. Billy Cooks was killed, the police said he reached under a pillow for a gun. Snappy McNeal was getting a lot of ink as one of the "Mag 7, the Kings of ghetto crime," but he wasn't charged.

Now as he drove toward Mobile Alabama, knowing that Snappy was as dead as Billy Cooks, John played a guessing game: Who is stronger than a "King of ghetto crime" an "Emperor?" Who could Snappy have given up? John's answer was simple. I don't know.

TEN

On the road of between Mobile and the Florida border, John started to think about Jose Diego Vargas. It was that case that had kept John working late in his office when Billy Cooks showed up.

John had been doing nothing but criminal defense since he left the Boggs firm. After working together for a year, where John had his own cases, worked on some of Steve's, and paid rent, John and Steve became partners. Along the way, John made the acquaintance of a Mexican chiropractor named Arthur Seguro.

Seguro had been a police officer for a couple of years for a small city police department near San Diego before he went to chiropractic school. He worked his way through school repossessing cars. Seguro would sometimes refer a criminal case—mostly arising out of his connections with people who cross the border for a living. Sometimes Arturo would refer a civil case usually an auto accident and Steve would handle it. While about half of Steve's practice was criminal work, it was obvious he would rather arrest most of his clients than defend them.

John found it amusing that while Steve still didn't like his clients—whether he had them in a civil rather than criminal matter—he seemed to find it easier making money off their supposed aches and pains than finding a reason for them not to go to jail. John would occasionally quip. "Steve doesn't like them any better, but he can be 'civil' with them."

Arthur Seguro liked John and wanted John to handle personal injury cases. One day at lunch, Seguro told John that he was planning to open another office, maybe two and that he would like to refer his cases to him. He didn't mind that Steve handled the few he sent over now, but if John would handle the cases himself he would send more— "much more." John told him he would think about it. As an afterthought Seguro mentioned that he had gotten a call from his former secretary as he was on his way to meet John.

"She was looking for the name of a good lawyer. I told her I was late for lunch with the best lawyer," he smiled. "And I gave her your name. "Her name is Maria Vargas. It is something about her brother. I was in a hurry and didn't ask her what kind of trouble he was in."

When John got to the office, he found that Maria Vargas had called and made an appointment to come in that afternoon. Maria came in with her sister Rosa. John guessed both women to be in their early twenties. They were neatly dressed. The story they told sounded impossible but it was obvious they believed it. John decided to check it out.

They told John that their brother Jose had just been convicted of a murder he did not commit. John had heard the claim of innocence before but usually it was from a defendant, who could not admit that he was capable of doing something wrong, or from someone who blindly believed what a loved one in trouble had said. What was different here was that these two young women had sat through the trial.

Both agreed that there were no witnesses who could put their brother, Jose, at the scene of the crime. According to the girls, all the witnesses agreed they saw only two men. One man had been shot and killed at the scene. Of the five witnesses four of them said that the robber who shot the store owner was Leon Ramos, who was arrested with their brother, Jose. But Ramos had testified at the trial that it was self-defense, that he had been in the store looking to buy beer and only shot the store owner when the store owner went crazy and killed his friend. He then drove to Jose Vargas's house to use the telephone because the gun he had dropped at the scene was registered to his brother, Hector Ramos. He wanted to call the police and tell them that the gun had been stolen because, with his record, he didn't think anyone would believe it was self-defense.

Ramos woke Jose up, but Jose's phone had been disconnected, so he went with Leon to a Laundromat to use the pay phone. The girls told John that their brother had never been in trouble before. At the trial he testified that on the morning of the murder he was asleep when Ramos woke him up and told him that Ramos's brother's gun had been stolen. He didn't ask Ramos any questions and when Ramos wanted to use the phone to call the police, he told him that it was disconnected. He walked with Ramos to a phone booth at the Laundromat and a police car came by. He saw Ramos get into the police car and the policeman asked him to get in too. He got in and went back to sleep. Then he was arrested for murder. The girls had come to John because the jury just convicted both Leon and Jose.

John took the girls' number and told them he would do some checking and get back to them to tell them if he would take the case. John's first move was to call the deputy Public Defender who had just lost the case. John was used to having people tell him their side of the case only to find out the evidence was quite different.

Not this time. The attorney confirmed what the sisters had told John and said he still couldn't figure out how he lost it. He would have no problem with John coming in and picking up the pieces.

John also called the probation department and spoke to the officer who was preparing the report for the probation and sentencing hearing. He told John that Jose had no prior record. He also said, "From what I can see the kid is innocent, but I can't put that in my report when the jury says guilty of first-degree murder."

John went to see Jose Vargas in the county jail. He found him to be a bright quiet young man. When they spoke about his background John was impressed by the fact that the young man had had a job that he was laid off from at the time of the murder and was worried about losing his job if he couldn't get out of jail in time to get back to work when the workers were called back in. John came away from the jail with the feeling that there was a massive injustice being done. He knew that he would be on the right side in trying to undo it.

One thing that Vargas said had stuck with him. Vargas had said that sometimes he felt like hitting someone but he just didn't know who.

John walked back to his car in the jail parking lot thinking, "Really, who do you hit. When the system gets this far off the track, who do you blame?"

He called the Vargas sisters and told them he would take the case. He didn't tell them, but in a way, he was looking forward to it.

After the fee arrangements were made the first step was to get the transcripts. Since it was a murder trial, they had been transcribed daily instead of waiting for the end of the case. John went to Compton where the case was heard and picked them up. There was close to three thousand pages in eleven soft covered volumes. Most of it was double spaced "Q" and "A" stuff so the reading went fairly quickly.

The case was set for a probation and sentence hearing and John was also going to make a motion for new trial before that "P & S" hearing.

John brooded about what he knew of the case so far. There didn't seem to be enough evidence to justify an arrest. Yet Vargas was arrested. Well, then you would expect the judge at the preliminary hearing to see that there was no case and kick the kid loose if the cops and the Deputy DA who filed the complaint didn't have their heads screwed on right. But no, the judge at the prelim passed the buck up the line figuring someone will let this kid loose, but it isn't going to be his neck.

When the case got to Superior Court the PD made a motion to re-examine the case that was presented to the prelim judge. The judge that heard that motion also said the case was really weak but he would give the prosecutor a chance to present a stronger case at trial. He was sure that they could not get a conviction with what they produced so far.

But the case at trial did not get any better. There was no witness who identified Jose. Of the five eye witnesses at the scene four said they were sure it was Ramos and the other said he didn't have any idea who it was. When the police searched, they found his fingerprints in the store, and they found scratches on his arms and hands that made it look like he had been hit by the glass that was shattered when his crime partner was shot near the store window. Jose had none of his fingerprints inside the store.

John thought he had to be missing something. He read through the transcripts again.

John was all set for the motion for new trial when Steve, who was on vacation when John got the case, came back. John had already read through the transcripts twice and some parts more than twice. John was convinced the prosecutor had not proved anything with regard to Jose other that he was with Ramos after the murder. When John told Steve about the case, he said he felt like telling the judge he was sure there had to be another volume of the transcript one he hadn't gotten— the one in which the prosecutor proved his case! Steve, who hadn't seen John this fired up since they met, warned John not to be too sarcastic. The judge Belsworth Reame was new to Superior Court and might still be suffering from judgeitis— that disease that makes a judge think he's as infallible as God.

John tried as best he could to heed the warning, but this case stirred something inside him. When he found himself discussing the case, he was amazed when he heard the forcefulness of his words. He realized that he was tired of just getting by and going along. He was tired of just being in court to hold someone's hand while they pled guilty. He would have happily sent most of his business to the Public Defender but when he discussed those feelings with Marsha she could only focus on the loss of income.

When John appeared in court beside Jose Vargas, he was prepared with his motion for new trial like he had not been prepared for a long time. He had always been well prepared in court; he was that rare combination of the lawyer who is good on his feet and also put in the time with the books. For this appearance John was prepared with a passion. He knew the record better than the judge, the prosecutor and Ramos's attorney who had all sat through the trial. John knew if he lost here the battle took on a much steeper slope. He knew by law that the trial judge, on a motion for new trial, is the last judge to have the power to reweigh the evidence—that is to look at it to determine if he is convinced beyond a reasonable doubt. Lawyers used the phrase, "on the motion for new trial the judge sits as a thirteenth juror." If you can convince him that he has a doubt you win your motion. Any judge who looked at the case after today could only decide if there is any rational basis for the decision that was made by those who weigh the evidence. John's research was full of cases in which the appellate courts reiterated the test—it was not their job, they would say, to determine if the defendant was guilty or not guilty, rather their job began and ended with a determination that those who could decide had some reasonable basis for the decision even if others could have come to a different decision given the same set of facts.

As John came into the courtroom the Public Defender met him and told him that Reame "looked shocked" when the jury returned the verdict of "guilty" against Jose Vargas. But he quickly balanced the "good news" with the "bad news" that the judge had made a comment that he would have to be reversed on this case.

The clear indication that he was prepared to join the long line of people who washed their hands as Jose Vargas got closer and closer to a life in prison.

John, after the formality of "substituting in" as the attorney for Vargas instead of the Public Defender, made his presentation.

The judge sat back and listened. Then he took John by surprise. The judge spoke directly to the prosecutor and declared that while he, the judge, had a decision to make, the prosecutor also had a decision to make. The prosecutor's decision, the judge continued, was whether he wanted to retry the case now or wait for it to come back from the appellate courts.

His last words to the prosecutor were, "and they have a case with Vargas, that could have gone either way." After the prosecutor got over his surprise at being asked that question in open court, he stammered that he didn't think there was any error that needed to be worried about. John wondered if had he stayed with the DA's office if his view of justice would have been warped the same way that the views of these two county employees was warped.

John tried to drive home to the judge the fact that, by his own admission, the case could have gone either way and therefore he had to grant the motion for new trial.

John's motion and all the reason it possessed was met with one word, "denied."

That was all the judge said. No reason, nothing on the record to show an appellate court his reasoning, or lack or reasoning, just "denied."

John, having been a deputy DA, knew that some judges wouldn't go to the bathroom unless the DA told him it was OK. They always seem to be running for office even after they have just been reelected. They live by the motto: "You can never be too hard on crime." Or at least that's the motto they run on. They learn early that they would rather err on the side of guilt than take the heat of a "soft on crime" label come election time. This judge had all the symptoms. John could not believe he could be that heartless though—that was a new low.

The sentencing ritual was a routine matter as they usually are. John again put up an argument but he knew his audience by now. His argument was really for those who would read the record on appeal. There was no way of reaching the man on the bench. No way at all. The sentence was a forgone conclusion.

John knew that if the judge couldn't see that he was passing sentence on an innocent man, he sure as hell wasn't going to be convinced by John's detailed analysis of the probation statute that Jose Vargas was in fact eligible for probation on the facts of this case because of his previous clean record and the fact that there was no proof he used a weapon in this case.

John wondered if the man even understood what he was hearing. John sure understood what he heard from the judge. The sentence to state prison "for the term prescribed by law" translated to "life in prison" since that was the term that was prescribed for first-degree murder.

When Jose was taken from the courtroom, he told the judge he just sentenced an innocent man.

As John left the court, those words ran through his mind. "An innocent man." John really didn't think in terms of innocent or guilty. He thought in terms of guilty or not guilty. He was annoyed every time he read in the paper or saw on TV that so and so "plead innocent" or worse "was found innocent." John, didn't feel comfortable describing Jose as an innocent man. At least not at first. At first, all he knew was that he wasn't proven guilty; certainly, not beyond a reasonable doubt.

John said goodbye to Jose's sisters. He knew, after all, they had expected no better. He had brought with him, and after the sentencing filed, the notice of appeal. His fee was based on making the motion and handling the appeal or retrial, but they all knew deep down it was going to have to go to appeal. John knew, as only experience can teach, that it was only his faith in the system that led him to believe that the motion for new trial had a chance. It was only the same faith in the system and his own need for this case that would sustain him in the years to come. With an "innocent" man sitting in prison, this was no ordinary case. This was going to have to be a crusade.

He went back to his office and set about converting the written motion for a new trail into the guts of the "Appellant's Opening Brief." Then, as he would from time to time, he went over the transcripts again to convince himself that Vargas was not in prison because John had missed something.

John found himself discussing the case with his friends more and more. He even got to the point of feeling sorry for Marsha who could almost repeat the story in his absence. From "civilians" the questions were always the same: how could something like that happen? John had asked himself the same thing when he first got the case and was still asking it every day.

He felt if the case came out of the Deep South of years back, or for all he knew even now, and Ramos and Vargas were Black, it would seem that the case was explainable if still not justifiable.

It was another guest at a party who suggested that being Mexican in Compton was damn near the same as being Black in Mississippi. John was hard pressed to give it any other explanation, so he chose not to dispute that one.

Eight months after Jose went to prison, the case was scheduled for oral argument in the Court of Appeal. The briefs had been filed by the Attorney General's office, who represented the People of the State of California on appeals from felony judgments; by the attorney the Court of Appeal had appointed to represent Ramos, who although he had retained an attorney for the trial had no more money and was allowed to have an attorney appointed to represent him now; and John.

The oral argument was the place to flesh out any areas that were not covered in the briefs.

John felt he had a good chance of convincing the court to reverse the judgment on some grounds. Every attorney with whom he had talked about the case told him that there was no way of them reversing on insufficiency of the evidence. It wasn't that they thought the case didn't demand it. They just felt no court was going to do it. John wondered if he was getting naive. He could not see how any court that understood what went on in this case could do anything but declare that the evidence could not support the jury verdict. But he took their warnings in stride and looked to raise other mistakes made by the trial court.

He was heartened when the case was assigned to a panel that included Franz Hess. He had read Hess's opinions and they indicated to John that this was a judge who had a keen mind; a judge who did not seem to have much patience with judges from the courts below his, who didn't have his vast legal knowledge.

It was late afternoon when it was John's turn to address the Court. Other than the court personnel, John and the deputy Attorney General assigned to the case where the only ones in the large courtroom. Leon Ramos's appointed attorney didn't think enough of his own case to appear, so he filed a statement to waive his oral argument. John assumed that the judges had read the record and the briefs that were filed. He felt compelled to point out that not only was the evidence at the trial insufficient but the evidence at the preliminary hearing was almost non-existent.

When John started his argument, Justice Hess interrupted him. "Counsel, I wonder if you could make this a little briefer, I'm worried about the time."

John was stunned. He answered without hesitation. "Your Honor, I'm worried about time too. My client has been sentenced to life in prison for a crime he did not commit. He has seven years to serve before he can even see the parole board. That is the time that I am worried about!"

Hess sat back in his chair. He nodded. "You've made your point," he said quietly. John continued his argument. He could not believe the judge's comment. He was only mildly pleased with his own. He thought his case was strong enough to withstand any damage his failing to "go along with the program" might have caused. Now he could only wait for their decision to be filed.

Then it was filed. When the opinion came, he ripped open the envelope.

Bad news.

The Court of Appeal unanimously affirmed the judgment of the Superior Court as to both defendants. He could not believe they would affirm Jose's conviction. When he read the opinion, he thought he was going to be ill. He could not accept this result. He had to call the Vargas family and break the news to them. But he also assured them he could not stop.

It was not going to be easy. The next step was trying to get the California Supreme Court to grant a hearing.

During the day, he went through his normal routine of court appearances. It was a blur of cases. John often felt like the man he had once seen in the circus who spins a number of plates and has to go back and make sure the first ones are still spinning when he adds others. This was a game John had gotten good at. The name of the game with guilty defendants is delay.

The old maxim that justice delayed is justice denied had long ago been modified by those who felt that justice delayed was just fine. The idea was to stall as long as possible and maybe get a break. Maybe the cop will go on vacation. Or a witness or victim would die or will move to Oregon, anything.

Then, when the string be stretched out no longer, the client pled guilty to something to remove the case from an overcrowded court calendar. The idea was to bargain the "year" the client was offered down to "six months." Or, try to get the "90 days made "straight probation." Anything to keep those who have done wrong from being punished for it. More and more John grew to dislike the stalling and haggling.

Sometimes the only bargaining power John had was that his crook knew something about a bigger crook. Often that was all that was needed. John used to think of the perpetual motion of having one of his clients "give up" someone else and then representing the newly created defendant while he turned in someone different. He and Steve used to kid about the implications of that type of system. Maybe even passing the cases back and forth so as not to appear to have a conflict of interest.

John however was becoming aware of another conflict. He was losing interest in doing anything but working on the Vargas case.

He would stay in the County law library until it closed. He knew he and Jose were down to their last court and that court had to be convinced to hear their case. Unless the Cal Supreme granted a hearing, that would be the end of the line for Jose Vargas. There was no hope of getting the case into the United States Supreme Court.

John filed his petition and waited. He called the attorney for Ramos to make him aware of what was going on. John hated waiting but he had adopted the philosophical position that if it was good news, it could wait and if it was bad news, he would hear about it soon enough. That the news was due to come by postcard was a fact that he thought was ironic.

He made another concession to desperation: before the section that contained the argument on the sufficiency of the evidence, he added a note. His prefatory note explained that he was well aware of the strictness and narrowness of that test, but he still felt that this was a case that would not meet that test no matter how narrow.

He thought about the propriety of that note while he waited. He hoped it would serve to focus an overworked reader.

About one week into waiting for the postcard, he was at his desk when the phone rang. Alone in the office, he answered it and sat upright in his chair when he heard the voice on the other end explain that he was the Clerk for the California Supreme Court.

He was calling to tell John that the Court had just granted a hearing.

John called Marsha and the Vargas family. He was elated. His mind raced. There was no need for the Cal Supreme to grant a hearing if they thought everything was properly decided.

After he had filed the petition, while he was waiting, he had done some research and found that the Court got about 2,000 petitions for hearing a year and in criminal cases granted 8%. About half of those were for the prosecution. John could not calculate the odds he had overcome just getting to where he was now. He started to feel that maybe things would work out after all. All he needed to do was keep studying and preparing for oral argument

The morning of the hearing, John met the Vargas family who had come to watch. He walked into the Courtroom and was struck by the sight of seven huge chairs in a line behind the raised bench. He sat and waited for the case to be called. One thing was sure. The would be no need for a discussion of "time."

When it came John's turn to argue he was as concise as possible. He made his points, answered the few questions that were asked by the judges and sat down. Now, all they had to do was wait. Again.

Three months after he appeared at oral argument, the opinion arrived in the mail.

They had won.

And to make it sweeter, the Court had decided it on the ground that everyone told John they would not touch. They had decided 5-2 that the evidence was insufficient to sustain the verdict. The court had reversed the judgment as to Vargas but affirmed the judgment as to Ramos. John called the Vargas family to tell them the news.

After discussions with the DA and the prison, John drove up to the prison with Jose's sisters and Jose Vargas was free.

The next day John appeared in the Inglewood Municipal Court on a drunk driving case. No one knew him there except his client. He had just won the biggest victory in his life. He had saved an innocent man from life in prison. John looked around the courtroom as though he was seeing the place with new eyes. He thought, Well, what did you expect, trumpets? A herald to run down the hall yelling John Street is coming?

He found his client. John, cornered the young deputy DA as he came into the courtroom with his arm loaded with files and waited while he and set his files down on the desk. John felt like he had jumped the line that would soon form. The kid DA was a bit abrasive John thought. John worked out a deal. John sat with his client. The charge of drunk driving would be reduced to reckless driving and his client would plead guilty. John knew that was how the game was played. He knew it was played that way for a simple reason. The charge of drunk driving is what he called a "priorable charge." That is on the second offense of drunk driving there is mandatory jail time. The way to avoid the second offense of drunk driving was not to get convicted of the first offense. So, his client's pled guilty to reckless driving instead of drunk driving.

As John looked at his watch, he could see it was 9:15 a.m. as he smelled the alcohol on his client. As he sat there, John knew his client had to "fortify" himself to face his day in court. John looked at his file and checked the client's address. As he waited, he calculated the distance the client had to drive to get to court. He wondered if anyone had ever been arrested for drunk driving while on the way to court to plead guilty while charged with drunk driving.

John watched as a line formed to talk to the young deputy. It was almost automatic, yet it was as though John was seeing the ritual for the first time. John watched this young punk hold court: he'd listen, then look in his file as though he was making sure the lawyer had not just made up the whole story, and then he said yes or no. The bartering was about money and time. How much of a fine if the client doesn't go to jail? Is this assault worth 90 days or six months? What do the cops say? At one point one of the older hands at the game had spoken to the cops first, he knew them better than the kid did. The kid told him that he represented the People of the State of California not the police. He knew he could say it. The cops weren't around to hear it.

John sat and watched as the line of attorneys, that used to lead to him when he was the prosecutor, snaked around the clerk's desk through the low swinging doors of the "bar" area and up the center aisle of the spectator section.

John couldn't wait to get out of there.

His client pled guilty, paid a two hundred and fifty dollar fine, and they both left. John felt empty. He had looked forward to winning a case like the Vargas case. Then he had won. But he was back at the spinning-the-plate game. The game he knew he hated.

He had to drive downtown to continue a jury trial that had been continued four times before. As he drove, he wondered how else he could make a living. There was nothing else he was trained to do. What he did know was that he could not discuss it with Marsha. After all their time together, he knew that she could not start over with him. She could not scale down their lifestyle while he retrained or looked for work that might be more satisfying to him.

That night John and Marsha were in bed watching television. They saw a nationally known lawyer on a talk show. He was bemoaning the condition of our criminal justice system. He told the audience; "If the judge makes a mistake and applies the wrong law, you can get that reversed on appeal. But if the jury makes a mistake and they convict someone they shouldn't, you can't get that reversed on appeal."

He turned to Marsha, "You see what I've been talking about? How hard it is to win on that ground. He is almost correct, but I won one!"

Marsha sat up. "Do you see what I have been talking about, John? He can't win one, you did—but yet you're here watching him on television!"

For an instant he realized that while he wanted to get out of the plate game, Marsha's answer would be to spin more and bigger plates. For the first time he wondered what she must think about being married to him. She wanted more money, yet he was not going to take out ads in the paper. Arthur Seguro, who still wanted John to think about personal injury cases, had called to congratulate John and tell him that he should have Jose go on Mexican TV to drum up some business. John had been amazed at the idea. Within the limits of what he felt was proper for a lawyer, he thought he was making a decent living and now maybe word of mouth would make it better.

Lying in bed, he did think of one way that he would not find improper and yet might generate the kind of money that would give him time to see what else he might want to do. On the ride home from prison Jose had said that he wanted to sue the police. John wasn't sure what kind of a civil case Jose could bring but he thought he could learn and even if he referred the case, he could do it on the basis that the new lawyer would have to split the fee with him.

On the ride home, Jose said he would call in a couple of days to talk about a possible false imprisonment or civil rights suit. John didn't see any evidence that Jose's civil rights had been violated. There was no more evidence of that than there was of his guilt. It was just one of those cases where the system broke down. But John knew that unless they could find a way to make it appear that what had happened to Jose was planned by someone, Jose would get no compensation for the time he spent in prison. He had told Jose he would do some checking and try to have an answer for him when he called.

Two days later Jose's sister Maria called to tell John that Jose had hired a flashy civil rights lawyer with a lot of political connections, William Wade Diamond. The lawyer had called Jose and promised that he would get him over five million dollars. Maria seemed embarrassed to be telling John the news.

As he they spoke, John tried to cover up his feeling of having been betrayed.

He never heard from Jose or his sisters again. But he did hear from his partner, Steve.

Steve said, "OK, so you had your biggest win. Great job! A few more like those and we can go broke. Did you ever stop to figure that with all the time you put into that case you maybe made ten bucks an hour? I know you didn't slack off on our other work, but jeez John—"

Two years later John read that Jose had settled with the city of Compton for three and one half million dollars. Now, unlike when he got Jose out of prison, there were newspaper headlines, based on the press release the attorney's office put out about the settlement and how Jose had been released from prison. None of the articles mentioned John's name.

John did a mental calculation of what the fee might be on a 3.5-million-dollar settlement. He knew that typically the attorney who refers the case to the attorney who represents the client gets a referral fee of a third of the legal fee. He wondered what Jose was going to do with his money. John knew he had no claim on it but on the ride home from the prison Jose had said that he knew he would still be in prison if it were not for John.

He would not stoop to contacting Jose, but—John imagined a call from Jose saying he wanted to give John a present. He wondered if in fact he did get a present like that what he would do with it. He wondered if that money could have gotten Steve and Marsha off his back.

That call never came.

Six months after reading about the settlement, Steve came into John's office to tell him the he had heard on his car radio coming back to the office that Jose had been shot and killed in a raid by the police in Hollywood.

ELEVEN

John was stunned by the news of Jose's death. William Wade Diamond, who Jose had hired for his civil rights case against Compton was now all over the media threatening lawsuits on behalf of the family. He claimed the killing was retribution by LAPD for Jose having made brother officers in Compton look bad. John and Steve watched part of an interview on the TV set in Steve's office.

Steve said that after 20 years as a cop and 20 as an attorney he had never heard so much bullshit in his live. Steve laughed and told John that he had seen "WWD" in court one morning. "A bunch of the guys where in old Morty Williams chambers. You remember old Morty used to like to take everybody into chambers at once rather than one at a time."

Steve looked to him. When he nodded that he had been in on those sessions, Steve continued. "Anyway, a whole group of us are in there and 'Dub-Dub' walks in. He clears his throat and without looking to see if anybody else is talking Dub-Dub says 'Your Honor—' Old Morty knows who the voice belongs to and he swivels his chair around to him and puts up his hand like a traffic cops and yells, 'Wait a minute counsel. Wait just a minute.' He reaches into his lower desk draw and pulls out this green and brown can. The label says 'Bullshit repellent!' Morty puts it on his desk between him and Dub-dub, sits back, folds his arms across his chest and says 'Counsel, now you may proceed.' You should have seen the look on Dub-Dubs face. That dirt bag never had a sense of humor. He never liked it when he found out all the guys made fun of his initials by calling him Dub-Dub. Old Morty never liked pompous assholes. When he put that can on his desk, I swear I thought Dud-Dub was going to explode."

After watching the news, John told Steve that he'd appreciate getting the low down on just what did happen in the apartment when Jose was killed. Steve knew after all the work for the impossible win, John had a special feel about the case. He said he'd check into it.

The next day Steve had his information. "The cops have been pushed real hard to show some results in the 'War on drugs" shit. They are working hard on this Black hooker who has a pad in Hollywood. They see her around with some heavy dirt bags. Then somebody comes up with a tip that the reason this two-bit hooker is seen with all these high steppers is because they have a safe in her closet with a lot of stuff and money in it."

"So, what's the Jose connection?" John asked impatiently.

"Well like I say the guys are taking a lot of heat. One of them comes up with the idea that they forget all this probable cause bullshit. They just kick down the door and if there is a safe there with drugs and shit they'll lose the bust in court but take a lot of shit off the streets and that will have to do for the time being. So, they get together a team and they kick the door. Your dummy is there on the couch. Mike Lucas from Hollywood detectives comes in with a shot gun and tells your guy and the hooker to freeze. Your guy looks at him and reaches under the pillow. When his hand comes up with something shinny Mike blows him away. What he came up with was a fucking cigarette lighter."

"What?" John was amazed.

"Hey I'm just telling you the way it went down. We don't know why the fuck your dummy was there in the first place. We don't know how he knows this sleazy chick. I mean he is fully dressed and she is in the other room when the thing goes down. Lucas says there was a strange look on your guy's face. Like he knew that if he moved Lucas was going to shoot and he moved anyway."

John said, "Well you would think after doing time in the joint he would know the game, if someone holding a shot gun says don't move—you don't move. What about this helping out the buddies from Compton bullshit?"

Steve shook his head. "That's all it is—bullshit. They didn't know your guy was in the apartment and they didn't know who he was until it was all over. Pure and simple, they've got no idea why he was there and why he reached when he did. Look if they executed this guy, they would have at least said he had a gun. And if it was like the old days, they would have brought a throw-down gun with them."

John had heard many of the "old days" stories. Of what it was like to be a cop in Los Angeles when Steve was on the job. Steve seemed in the mood to talk and John was in the mood to listen.

Steve looked as though he was reluctant to start the story then gave a what-the-hell shrug and began.

"One time my partner and I had busted this creep on a robbery. I mean we had him dead bang. Some wacko judge just cut him loose. We couldn't believe it. Well, this robber starts calling us up and making all kinds of threats.

He's going to sue for false arrest. We messed with the wrong guy this time, blah blah blah.

"I mean most guys when they catch a break know enough to drift into the woodwork. The last thing they want to do is make waves, right? Well sure enough we make him on another robbery—same MO, description fits him, everything. We go out to pick him up. We get to the door and this guy is talking all kinds of trash. He's a big guy and he's yelling he's going to kick our asses. Then he's going to take our houses away, we are going to get fired with no pension, everything we've worked for we're gonna lose. He'll see to it that we never work again. Our families will have to go on welfare. He turned to my partner and starts screaming this shit at him. He raised a fist and turned to me real fast and he went down."

Steve looked at John for a reaction.

John made a motion like he was waiting for the rest of the story.

Steve continued, "In my mind I was protecting myself and my partner from a raving nut robber. But we knew that some citizens might not see it that way. Don't get me wrong I'm not proud of what I did. But it was done. My Sergeant shows up, and he sees the guy down there with one hole in the chest.

"He says, 'He had a gun.'

"I said, 'Sarge I don't know about a gun. He raised his fist and came real fast and—'

"He says, 'I'm not asking you, I'm telling you he had a gun. That's the way it went down.' He takes a gun out of his pocket and drops it near the guy and says, 'Look, here it is.' Then he winks at me and says he has to call the shooting team."

Steve looked at John again. He sighed, "If the guys I spoke to in Hollywood wanted to clean all this shit up they wouldn't have had your dummy come up with a cigarette lighter. There are enough guns around not to need no fuckin cigarette lighters. Besides, I know this Lucas. He's a good clean cop. Your boy just didn't follow the rules."

Steve stood up and put his hands on his lower back and stretched backward. "I'm getting more tired of this law bullshit with each day. I'll see you tomorrow after court."

John knew exactly how Steve felt. With Steve doing twenty years as a cop followed by twenty years as a lawyer, John knew that Steve was looking for the day he could call it quits.

On his ride home from the office, John tried to put together the pieces of the puzzle. He could not.

It sounded to him that Jose wanted to commit suicide. It would be too much to imagine that he knew there would be a raid and put himself in harm's way. That would be almost impossible. But what was possible, was to think it was a choice to do the wrong thing once he was in the wrong situation.

Thinking about it on his ride home that day, John wondered if, that was exactly what Jose had done. There was of course the other possibility. That Jose had not reached for anything at all—that the "he reached and I reacted" was an after the fact lie.

But John trusted Steve's instincts on that. No, it must have been that for some reason Jose wanted it to be over.

John wondered about what might cause Jose to want it to be over. He had his money. But, then John thought maybe that was it. Maybe the thing that John thought would make Jose want to live was what made him want to die.

John remembered how empty he had felt after winning the Vargas case. Not only because he did not get a shot at the referral but because after he achieved what he had set out to achieve, his life did not seem to be any better. In a way it seemed a little worse.

At least when he had the goal of getting Vargas out of prison he had that goal, a target—something to aim at. Shortly after he won, John wondered what he could aim at next.

John wondered if Jose was feeling the letdown of having achieved what he wanted and still finding himself the same person when he woke up the next day. John also wondered if Jose felt any remorse for the way he had forgotten about the man who got him out of prison.

He realized that he had no idea what was going on with Jose in the years since he got him out. In any event, Jose was dead. John was not sure how he felt about it. He knew now that he was not going to get a call from Jose wanting to share his wealth. He knew a chapter in his life was over.

In the stories of Jose's death all John saw were the references to the settlement with Compton. Nowhere did John see the mention of his name as the lawyer who got Jose Vargas out of prison.

John had been working on Jose's case the night Billy Cooks had visited him. John had mentioned working on Jose's case while waiting in court with Betina Swift.

About three weeks after Jose's death, the heat that caused the police to break down the door to the apartment where Jose was killed, caused the arrest of someone who was high up in the pecking order just below Mag 7.

One week later, John got the call from Snappy Mc-Neal.

TWELVE

It was pouring when John saw the sign that told him he was entering Jacksonville. The combination of the gloomy weather, terrible driving conditions, and fatigue caused him to have a "That's nice—so what?" attitude when he saw the sign that said "End 10 exit one mile."

John had a new decision to make. North? South? Or stay put for a while? As tired as he was, the decision was really easy. It was winter and John didn't want to deal with the cold weather. He would drive off the last exit on 10, get a place to stay for the night, and then drive south.

John went to sleep thinking about Marsha and Steve. He wondered what things had been like for them in the past ten days. He wondered if he had made a mistake. He wondered if he would be able to keep up his resolve to stay "dead."

He was wondering as he fell asleep.

The next morning the sun was shining. John looked at his watch it was already 10:30. He called the desk and extended his check out time to one o'clock. He got up took a shower and, for the first time on his trip, went back to bed. When he woke again at 12:30 he was surprised that he had been able to sleep again.

He realized that he must have really needed the sleep, that he had been pushing himself very hard. He thought he might just stay another night, but decided to get back on the road.

When he got to Miami that evening, he seemed drawn to the airport area. He thought perhaps because he had flown into Miami once with Marsha on their way to a cruise ship vacation. That was the only explanation he could give himself for his decision to look for an apartment in that area. It looked to be an older area with some single-family houses still standing among the newer two-story stucco apartment buildings. He saw a building with a "for rent" sign. The wide street reminded him of the street he grew up on south of Los Angeles. He took a chance that it was not too late and knocked on the door of the manager. The young woman showed him a second-floor apartment. There was a pool in the center or courtyard area. When John was going up the interior outdoor stairs, the manager, motioning toward the pool, pointed out that being so close to the airport they got a lot of young singles who worked for the airlines.

The scene, as he looked down from the open railed-in area on the second floor, reminded him of the LA singles scene, even to the palm trees. When the manager asked what he did for a living, he lied and said he was a crime reporter on a paid sabbatical so he could write his novel.

He took the apartment.

John had started making mental notes of the things he saw as he traveled across the country. He had even scribbled a line or two of a poem. He thought that now that he had the time, he might try his hand at writing. He was also aware that the money would not last forever and that he would have to think of some way of making a living when it ran out. If he got to the point of publishing anything he could always use a pen name.

John spent the next few days furnishing his new place. He wasn't sure how long he was going to stay in the area.

So, he went to yard sales and thrift shops to get his furniture knowing that he could sell it or leave it without hesitation if he wanted to get back on the road.

After making a purchase in a thrift store, he smiled when he remembered the furnishing of his home with Marsha. He had just furnished his whole apartment for what she had paid for an end table she just had to have. He did splurge on two items though. He did get himself a good small stereo and good portable TV. He rationalized that he could always take them with him whenever he decided to move on.

Within a week he had his smattering of used furniture. He had an old king size bed that took up most of the bedroom. He had not really thought about the size of the bed when he bought it. He liked the way it looked and it was cheaper than the smaller beds the Salvation Army Store had. One piece of his "furniture" that looked out of place was the spare tire from the car.

John had decided that was going to be his bank. He kept the cash in the deflated tire and he put the tire, wheel and all, on a milk box. He covered it with a board the same size and shape as the tire, then put a cloth over the whole thing, and placed the TV on it. John thought no one would ever figure there was over $140,000 in the tire. They might steal the TV but the tire-table would not be dragged out of the apartment and down the stairs even on a bet. He also bought a small couch and an old Formica kitchen table with metal legs and the three chairs that matched. Looking around his new home, John laughed when he thought what Marsha would say if she saw his apartment. He thought, If I wasn't already dead, she would kill me.

After having half-furnished the apartment he found himself staying home a lot. There were stretches of time that he would only go out to shop for food or to get another magazine to read. His days were spent reading, sleeping, or watching TV.

Finally, one evening he got angry with himself after having fallen asleep watching television. He got down on the floor and tried to do some push-ups. He got to four. That made him more unhappy. It looked too cold to go down to the pool so he settled for a shower. He shaved for the first time in a week and went out.

He wasn't sure where he was going but he had to go out. He thought he'd find a movie or maybe just explore the neighborhood. When he got to the car, he remembered he had seen a place called Lady's Lounge a few blocks away. He decided to walk over and check that out.

When he walked into the parking lot, he could see that the place was much bigger than he had realized when he had first passed it. He walked in the door and to his left was a bar and to the right a restaurant area separated from the bar by a low wooden barrier with a neck-high glass rectangular top.

He sat at the bar, ordered a beer, and watched the people around him. The restaurant area had twelve tables. The bar had ten stools. He had been in the place for about an hour, and was working on his third beer when he saw a beautiful dark-haired woman, in a tasteful, loose fitting, belted at the waist dress, walk in with a much shorter, well-tailored man who appeared to be Japanese. With her high heels, she towered over him. John could not take his eyes off her as she slid into her seat at the corner table. As the waitress came over to offer the couple drinks, John realized he was tired enough to head home.

The next night he went back and took the same seat at the bar. He struck up a conversation with the bartender: a short, husky, Canadian named Randy. Soon after John told his crime reporter lie, Randy related that he had played minor league hockey and two years for a college team but after a shoulder injury ended his scholarship and his hockey days, he and a friend, a former minor league teammate, had drifted down to Florida. Listening to Randy speak about Harvey, John was just getting the message that Randy and Harvey where a couple when Lady, the owner, came over and asked if John wanted another beer on the house.

He spent the evening talking with Randy and Lady between their taking care of the other bar customers. They were starting to become friendly. He looked at his watch and was just getting ready to leave when he saw the woman who had been there the night before with what John had taken for Japanese man, walk in with a giant of a coal black man in a black and gold African dashiki. They headed for the same corner table. John gave Randy a "do-you-see-what-I-see?" look but Randy just smiled and toweled off the top of the bar.

John tried not to stare but he was intrigued by this woman. When she got up from her seat and walked on the restaurant side of the separation wall to the lady's room, she nodded at Randy though the glass and he smiled and said, "Hi T."

John looked at Randy but saw that even though he knew the woman, there was no more information he was going to give. Changing his mind about leaving, John ordered another beer. When the woman walked back to her table, she smiled at John.

He turned to Randy and said, "OK. I got it. She's some kind of official with the United Nations."

Randy smiled, "You could say that. But I'm not sure how official it is."

She was still at her corner table when John went home.

The next afternoon John decided to go for a walk and do more exploring of his neighborhood. It was about four thirty and he was on his way back when he decided to stop in at Lady's. As he entered, he could see a woman in jeans, a sweatshirt and flip-flops with her back to him sitting in the seat he had occupied the last two nights. She was leaning over the bar talking quietly with Randy.

When John took another seat, she turned to him and said, "Oh. Am I in your spot?"

John realized it was the girl he had seen before. He was deciding if he should call her "T" and say,"No T it's OK," when she got up saying, "I know how territorial men can be," and sat down one stool over gesturing that the seat was now his.

He had no special attachment to that stool, but since she got up so he could have it, he sat down. She spun toward him on her new stool, and stuck out her hand, "Hi, I'm Carla."

"I'm John."

"I was just leaving. Randy, give John his usual beer on me."

Randy was delivering the beer as John watched her leave.

He saw the look on John's face and chuckled, "Here's your beer. You're here early."

John started to play along, "Well if I would have known that she—" But, stopped, "OK, so you called her

T and she introduces herself as Carla, should I switch my fantasy of her employer from the United Nations to the CIA?"

"Your fantasy would be wrong either way. Her name is Carla but when she's working, she is Tione. Sounds like a tie you own"

He smiled. "Tione gives the complete girlfriend experience."

Randy let that sink in, then chuckled, "Don't even think about it. You probably couldn't afford Tione and Carla doesn't like men."

John sat there thinking about her and some of the "working girls" he had known as he nursed his beer.

Later that night, John walked back to Lady's and took his usual seat and at the bar and was there when Tione came in with another man and took her corner seat.

THIRTEEN

Marsha was just waking. She had to get up. It was hard. She wasn't used to getting up early but she realized she needed to get into shape. Before getting out of bed, she reached over to the end table and put another message on the small note pad, "Call Steve to check on household money."

It was still too early to call Steve so Marsha decided to take a shower. She looked at herself in the mirror. She ran her hand down her thighs and made a mental note that she should get back to riding her exercise bike.

Karen called while Marsha was still wet. They spoke for about 20 minutes. Karen wanted Marsha to go out with her that evening. Karen told her it would be good for her. Marsha was surprised by the idea and a bit annoyed but said that she would think about it and call her back.

After three weeks without John, Marsha didn't feel like she was ready to go out just yet and wondered why her friend didn't see that.

Marsha called Steve. Her household account was running low, and she wanted to know just what her financial situation was going to look like. He told her that it would take some time for the insurance situation to be sorted out but that for now at least she didn't need to worry. John had about $3500 in his office account and Steve would transfer that to the joint account that Marsha could write checks on. And a couple of checks just came in, amounting to about $2000 and Steve would put those in the account as well.

He laughed and told her that he was getting good at signing John's name. Marsha again thanked him for taking care of everything for her.

Before Marsha could call Karen back Karen called again. She wanted to be more pushy about the evening.

Karen said, "There is a place I heard about that is supposed to have a nice relaxed atmosphere and I want to check it out. I think it would be good for you to get out of the house. It's been a month already, hasn't it?"

"Just about, more like three weeks"

"Well, what are you going to do if you don't go?"

"I don't know. You want us to go out and meet men," she said accusingly.

"Who me? Meet men? What I want to do is go out and see people and hear live music. I like doing that. Yes, there may be some men there doing the same thing. Like I said what are you going to do—sit home alone? Come on, just keep me company. You don't even have to enjoy yourself," she laughed.

Marsha surprised herself by agreeing to go along.

"Good! I'll swing by and get you around 8:30."

"Karen what do I wear to this kind of place?"

"Wear something comfortable. I hear the place is pretty relaxed. Besides, the odds on really meeting anybody at these places are slim so you might as well be comfortable. I'll see you at 8:30."

Marsha called Karen three more times before Karen arrived to pick her up. She wanted to check again as to what she should wear. Karen was amused at her Marsha's nervousness.

It was a side of her that she did not often see.

They went out around 9 p.m.

When they got back to Marsha's house it was one in the morning. They were comparing notes.

Marsha said, "You seemed to know several of the people at this place. I thought this was a place you were checking out for the first time?"

Karen reached down and took off her shoes. "It was, but you see many of the same people at these kinds of places. Sometimes they hop from one to another in the same night. I once ran into the same guy in three places in the same night. He accused me of following him."

"Were you?"

"No. He was at this place tonight, too."

"Which one was he?"

"He was the only one that didn't try to come on to you," Karen kidded.

Marsha smiled at the compliment. "You seemed to be doing all right for yourself. I couldn't belief that guy you were with on the dance floor though."

Karen smiled, "He wouldn't leave me alone. If he was going to be that aggressive if we were alone that would be one thing, but in a public place? I really thought he was going to try and have me right there."

"You don't think you kind of encouraged him?"

She shook her head, "I don't know. I was a little tipsy at that point I don't know what I wanted. He must have thought I wanted him right there."

"What about you. Did you give the guy with the dark glasses your phone number?"

Marsha smiled, "No, but another guy gave me his card and asked me to call him to have lunch some time."

"Well, it looks like you were pretty busy while I was away. Who gave you the card?"

Marsha looked through her purse and dug out the card. She handed it to Karen.

Karen read it and asked, "Do you think you'll call?"

"I don't think so. I'm not ready for that yet. Do you think I should?"

"I don't know. What does he look like?"

Marsha laughed, "I don't know officer he was wearing a mask and the room was dark.

"I'm starting to feel like I am back in high school, Karen. I'm not complaining it just feels that way."

"The difference is you can enjoy it more this time. And you don't have to worry about your reputation."

"Or homework," Marsha interrupted

Karen stayed for a while longer. Marsha offered her the guest room but Karen decided to head home.

That night Marsha thought about John and their life together. She thought about the club she and Karen had gone to and the guy who gave her his card. She fell asleep thinking about the band and the music.

The next morning Marsha was woken up by a shout. It seemed to be coming from the lawn in front of the house. She put on her robe and ran to the door. There was a man lying in her driveway. He was wearing a jogging outfit. He was on his back holding his leg. When Marsha opened the door, he looked up and saw her.

"Please, I've twisted my knee. Can you help me?"

"What do you want me to do?"

"If you can help me over to the steps and call my brother to come and get me, I'd appreciate it."

He looked to be about thirty and had a warm smile that was highlighted because of his tan complexion.

Marsha came down and helped him to the bottom step. He sat down and told her his brother's name and number. She made the call. The brother lived only a mile away and said he'd come right over.

Marsha went back out. "Do you want to come inside?"

"No thank you. I'll be OK here. If I went in, I'd have to come back out. Besides I'm all sweaty."

"I'll get you a towel. Would you like some water or orange juice?"

"Juice would be wonderful. Do you have any ice?

"I mean for my knee not for the juice. By the way, my name is Mathew. I'm sorry for the inconvenience. I appreciate your help."

"I'm Marsha," she smiled back.

She went in and came out with the towel and the ice and went back for the juice.

He dried himself off and then wrapped the ice in the towel.

"Is the leg very bad?"

"I don't think so. I'll get home and keep more ice on it."

"Do you want me to get some more ice now?"

"No that's OK besides my brother, Peter, is coming around that corner," Mathew said finishing the juice.

He pointed to a bright red sports car that was now stopping in front of the house.

Peter got out of the car. He came over, unwrapped the towel and looked at Mathew's knee. Peter thanked Marsha for all her help. He put his arm around Mathew's waist and helped him into the car.

Marsha followed them. She stood there holding the empty glass.

Peter looked at her. "Do you always look this great in the morning?" he asked.

Mathew glared at him.

"Hey, Mat I was just making conversation."

Mathew was embarrassed. He looked at Marsha. "Maybe next time I'll ask you to call an ambulance," he looked at his brother, "Maybe they can keep their mouths shut."

Marsha smiled. "No harm done. Maybe you should see a doctor."

Peter leaned over Mathew to the window. He grinned. "Pretty lady, we're both doctors!"

Mathew shook his head and shrugged his shoulders. He smiled at her as Peter drove away.

She watched as they left. She found herself following the car with her eyes until it was out of sight around the corner.

It was too early to call Karen so she decided as long as she was up, she would shower and get dressed. She waited until what she thought was a reasonable hour and called. She woke Karen up anyway.

Karen was fascinated. She, of course, wanted to hear about these doctor brothers. Marsha assured her that if she ever set eyes on Mathew again, she would see what she could do for Karen with "brother."

It was two days later, in the afternoon, when Mathew came back with the towel. When she heard the doorbell, Marsha was in the laundry room. When she saw it was Mathew at the door, she was embarrassed to be in sloppy clothes. He tried to put her at ease.

"I seem I have a way of dropping in and catching you at odd moments"

"That's all right. Come on in Mathew, she said motioning toward a couch, "How are you?"

"My brother says I'll live," he said sitting down.

"You needed a second opinion?" She sat on the other couch.

"No, but you can't treat yourself, it screws up the billing."

"Oh, I see," she laughed.

"I was going to ask what kind of doctor you and your brother are. Now I know—the billing kind."

He put up his hands. "Hold it. This has gone far enough. I'm an orthopedic surgeon. My brother is a specialist in emergency medicine. I am into sports medicine. By the way my last name is Scaldi. Maybe you heard the name in connection with some of the local teams. I'm the team doctor for a few of them."

"No, I can't say that I have. I don't follow sports."

She saw him look at her left hand, but knew that that wouldn't tell him anything. She hadn't worn her wedding ring in years.

He was tentative when he fished, "Well, maybe your husband has heard the name." She was glad she had seen the question coming. And even more glad that she knew why it was asked and that it was asked.

"Mathew my husband is missing, she paused, "and presumed dead. He went out sailing about a month ago and they never found a body."

"Oh. I'm sorry. I just wanted to know if—"

"I know why you asked and I'm pleased that you wanted to know." She smiled at him and he smiled back.

She sank back into the couch, and looked at his eyes. She saw that he too had settled back into the couch as though he was going to be there for a while. She was pleased but a little uncomfortable with the attention. She took a deep breath and thought of something else to talk about.

They talked for a couple of hours. Finally, she said she was going to make some dinner. She invited him to stay but he looked at his watch and realized he had stayed much longer than he thought he would.

When they walked toward the door, he said he had felt very comfortable talking to her. She said she felt the same.

That was all they said.

She made a mental note that if she saw him again, she had to find out about Peter for Karen. There would be time to fix up Karen and Peter.

It was two weeks before she heard from Mathew again. When he had said he felt comfortable talking to her, she had expected that she might hear from him sooner than that.

About the third day with no call, she began to wonder if she had misread him. After all she had not been in the dating scene for a long time. She didn't think she was there now, but could she have been that far off in her assessment. She spoke to Karen who advised her to call him. She couldn't do that. If he called her, she would go out with him. But for her to call a man, specially so soon after John's disappearance—

Karen's next suggestion was to just hang in. She was sure that Marsha could read people pretty well.

When Mathew did call, Marsha was pleased. One of the teams that he took care of was just finishing the season and there would be a big party at the home of the owner after the last game. He wanted to know if she would like to go.

Saying "yes" was so simple she thought afterward. The word was out before she even had realized it. Now as she hung up the phone the doubts hit her. What was she doing? Was it too soon? How would she know if it was or it wasn't?

She knew she wanted Mathew to call. She knew she would have felt hurt if he didn't. She knew she wanted to go to this party with him. She realized then that she had answered her own question. If she knew she wanted to go, it must be OK for her to go.

She forgot to ask which team and where the party was going to be. But he said he would call the next day with more details so she could wait.

The party was for the basketball team. He arrived to pick her up precisely on time. He was looking at his watch to check the time as she opened the door.

Marsha was pleased by the look in Mathew's eyes when he saw her. She had tried hard to look as beautiful and sophisticated as she could. It was not only their first date, but, she realized, the first time he had seen her in something other than the robe she wore when they met, or the sloppy jeans she had on while doing house work.

When they got in the car he asked her, for the first time, if she knew anything about basketball.

"I've seen the game on television once or twice. My husb— John once represented a player from one of the local schools who was accused of raping a girl at the school.

"Oh? Who was that? Was that recent?"

"It was two years or so ago. I don't remember the name. I'm not even sure that I ever knew it."

"What happened? Did the guy go to jail?"

"Oh, no." She said matter-of-factly. "In talking to the player, John found out that someone once tried to bribe him and a teammate to fix a game. John knew that the man involved with the game fixing was someone the police would be more interested in than his rapist. So, they made a deal. No time for the rapist in exchange for his cooperation on the case with the fixer. John was always good at taking care of his clients."

"What about the girls who was raped. What kind of a deal did they make with her?"

"I don't know. John didn't tell me everything about his business. He knew there was stuff he was dealing with that I would rather not know."

The party went on till two in the morning. Marsha was dazzled. She had expected a small party with some athletes she didn't know, but whose names she had been coached on by Karen. It turned out to be a big party with many famous Hollywood people attending. They were all fans of the team. The party was indeed at the home of the owner.

The home was a ranch in Malibu. Several acres on a hill overlooking the ocean. There was valet parking and a tram to take guest up the long narrow driveway from the parking area. There was a live big-name band.

Mathew drifted in and out of the groups of players and the groups of star fans. After getting a drink at the bar overlooking the ocean, Marsha stood watching the moon over the water. For an instant she thought of John and his sailing trip. But that instant was all she had to be reflective because Mathew asked her to dance.

As she walked, holding his hand, to the dance floor, she couldn't remember the last time she had danced.

She made a big hit with the players. Several of them came over the table where she and Mathew were seated to "dance with Doc's lady."

Mathew's brother, Peter, was there. He seemed to know several of the women at the party. One look at him in action told her that she could forget trying to set up Karen. Karen was attractive, but the good doctor seemed to be playing in a different league. But, then again, she would have to give Karen a shot if that is what she really wanted.

In the car on the way home, Marsha was curled up in the passenger seat. She felt that she had had a wonderful time. She was wondering what was going to happen next. Mathew didn't ask her anything about going to his place. It was obvious to her they were headed for her house. She wondered what was going to happen when they got there. She tried to think out what she wanted to happen. She couldn't.

She was attracted to him. She had no question about that. She didn't know if she could handle going to bed with him now. She wondered what would happen if she did. She wondered what would happen if she didn't. Before she knew it, they were at the house.

She unlocked the door wondering what she should do next. Standing just inside the door, he held his arms out and she folded herself in them. It was a nice long hug. She felt the warmth of his body and she felt herself relax. He rubbed her neck and gently massaged her shoulders. It was not an overt pass. It could have been the good-night hug of long-time friends. But she found herself responding by holding him tighter. He took her hand and took a few steps to his left and they were on the couch.

He kissed her.

She felt his hand go down her back as she leaned against him. She was kissing him deeply now. His hand went to her breast. She could feel the strength in his body.

Her passion surprised her. She decided to go with it. They made love on the couch quietly. After she had climaxed several times, she could feel him as he came inside her.

They lay in each other's arms almost fully clothed. She was pleased with herself and pleased with him. She felt awake and alive. She could feel her heart beating—pounding. Could he feel it? How could he not? He was quite different from John. He was younger, firmer, and stronger.

She was surprised that she was able to respond so fully. At one point in her marriage, she had wondered if she would be able to function with a man who did not know her body as well as John did. Now, she was surprised neither guilt nor shame nor Mathew's unfamiliarity kept her from getting aroused. She was pleased that they had not. She felt that she was fine, and that this thing between them was fresh and new. And she felt she wanted to do whatever he wanted her to do to keep him.

She picked her head up and looked at him. She thought of the evening they had just spent, and the time they had just shared like kids on the couch. She felt his body next to hers. Listened to him inhale and exhale softly next to her. She could still feel her heart pound as she put her head back down on his chest and kissed his hand and she moved his arm around her shoulders.

After a while, she sat up and put his head in her lap. She looked down at him and smiled. She stroked his head and his chest.

"I think I should warn you, Marsha. I'm a one-woman man. I don't like to juggle relationships. My brother does enough of that for the whole family. Although I don't think even he would call them relationships. I'm not like that. I don't have the time for that. Or I won't make the time. I like to find someone I like and stick with her. And, I think you might be stuck with me."

He left about dawn. She couldn't wait to call Karen. But she could not call her at dawn.

She fell asleep.

When Marsha called later that morning, Karen could hear the excitement in Marsha's voice as she told her about the party.

Karen said, "Hey, when we met, I used to think that you were the only one in LA who was not star struck, but now I know better

"Well—"

Karen said, "Well, I think you owe me an apology."

"What? Why?"

"Look, every time I saw someone famous and told you I just saw so and so, you always made me feel like a high school kid. Not that I'd mind being the age again, but you know what I mean. Now, to hear you go on—"

"Well—"

"Well, the difference dearest," Karen continued, "is that when I like something or someone I don't make a big secret of it."

"That's for sure!"

"Whereas you always seem to think that being cool is being better."

Marsha started to listen to her friend more closely. She realized that Karen was serious.

"But," continued Karen, "When you are excited about something or someone it shows. Maybe you thought you were cool and hiding it but I could tell what was going on."

"Karen, did you feel that I had put you down about the star stuff. I'm sorry if I made you feel that way. You're the dearest friend I have. I need you."

I need you. Was a simple three-word statement. It almost seemed to slip out. They both paused for a second to let it sink in.

Karen started slowly gathering her usual bravado. "If I had ever felt put down, I would have let you know. Like I said, I don't hide things very well. Now, some basic questions. Does he know that you're older than he is?"

"We discussed that. I'm 36 he's 32—he's says that's no problem. His mother is older than his father. In fact, we laughed that you would expect kids to be making out on the couch afraid of getting caught. I promised him we could use the bedroom next time."

"Does he know about your money situation?"

"What money situation?"

"Does he know that Steve thinks before the end of the year you are going to have a million dollars in insurance money?"

Marsha was stunned by the question. "We never discussed that."

"Well do you think there is any way he could know about it?"

"Do you mean do I think he is interested in me for my money? I never gave it a thought. Maybe it would be nice to have a man who thinks about having lots of money. Do you think I sound terrible? Do you think it is too soon for me to be thinking like this?"

Karen said, "First, I don't think it makes a difference what I or anyone else thinks. Next, I don't know what you mean by too soon. Do you mean not enough time since John or not enough time with Mathew? If you mean too soon after John. I guess the fact that Mathew asked you out and you accepted means it was time for you to move on with your life. If you mean too soon with Mathew. I don't know. I haven't even met him yet. But my advice is always the same. If it feels all right, go ahead and do it. There is plenty of time to worry about it later."

Marsha listened intently. "You know Karen, I guess I'll just have to take John's advice. John always used to say that you never wait until you're ready for some things because for some things you may never be ready. You do things when you have a chance to do it."

"I'll miss him." Karen said softly. "OK, now that I've said that—what is Mathew like in bed?"

Marsha laughed, "I don't know. We never got off the couch, but—"

She thought about the conversation for a long time after she hung up. She was truly glad she had told Karen that she needed her because she did. She thought about Mathew and there was no way he could have known about any insurance money. She pictured them together. She thought of the people he knew. The famous people who were at the party. She could feel the excitement of this new relationship within her. She felt warm and good.

FOURTEEN

John had been in Miami for over a month, and was becoming a regular at Lady's. One afternoon John was walking to a local bank to get ten of his one-hundred-dollar bills broken into smaller bills.

He didn't want to use his credit card and he didn't like the idea of always pulling out a C-note to pay for things. It made him stand out in a neighborhood of "working folk." The big bills made him think of his life on the coast.

Since most of his clients were in businesses that dealt in cash, that was how he was usually paid, although with the clients who were closer to the street trade, often he saw smaller bills. He knew that after a street dealer paid him in fives, tens, and twenties, that he himself was just an extension of the sale.

He and Steve would occasionally pocket a fee that was in cash and use it for what he called his walking-around-money or WAM for short. He would watch the other criminal lawyers in their expensive suits and flashy cars. He used to call them peacocks. He would watch the big bills roll out of their pockets, and see the big rings and the thick gold chains. He knew that you needed a lot of ego to take the pounding that a criminal lawyer takes on a daily basis, so he understood his "peacock brethren of the bar." John just didn't want to be one. There were times when he would feel flush and happy, usually when he had just won a tough case, and he would spend a couple of the big bills he had gotten, but that was very rare. Usually, most of the WAM went straight to Marsha.

As John was walking into the bank, he saw Randy and two Black men coming out. Randy had some bills in his hand. He saw John and beamed. "Hey old buddy how are you?"

John saw the two Black men uncomfortably glance at one another. He summed up the scene in a flash. Then, John wondered if he had jumped to the right conclusion.

He smiled at Randy. "Hi yourself, old buddy," he laid it on, "Who are your two friends." He watched the two men get more nervous.

"Oh, I just met these guys." Randy beamed.

John took a shot, "Was one of them looking for the Hotel on Peagreen St.?"

Randy was opening his mouth to say "yes" when he saw the two men turn and run down the block. Randy stared in disbelief as he watched them run around the corner.

He turned to John. "You want to tell me what the fuck is going on here?

"How did you know what that guy said to me?"

John tried to suppress his smile. He realized that Randy was upset because he wasn't going to make the killing he thought he was going to make. "Randy, the first guy, the one that asked you about the hotel, he had a Jamaican accent, right?"

"Well, he had some kind of accent, yeah. Go on."

John continued, "—and he asked about this hotel that you never heard of, right?" Randy didn't answer this time so John just went on.

"—and then this other guy shows up and they get into a conversation about this hotel. Then they start talking about banks," John smiled at Randy

"Stop me if I'm wrong. Then the first one pulls out a big roll and says his captain on his boat used to hold all his money for him and he paid the captain three thousand dollars to hold his money."

"Four thousand," Randy interrupted. Seeming pleased that he had the chance to correct John, but still puzzled.

"I'm sorry," smiled John "I didn't know that inflation had hit the captain-holding-money-business." He was pleased at his own joke. "—Anyway, he said the captain held his money because you couldn't trust banks. You could put your money in, but you couldn't get it out when you wanted. And you're angry at me because he was going to give you some money just for taking your money out of the bank so he could see that it could be done."

"Well, he was going—" Randy interrupted.

"What he was going to do," continued John, "is tell you to hold your money and his phony roll of bills—with a hundred-dollar bill wrapped around some play money— and put it all in a bag. Then he was going to watch you hide the money somewhere on your body. No matter where you put it, he was going to say that was no way to hide money.

"Then he was going to take the bag with your money and his phony roll and switch it with a bag of paper and shove the paper under your shirt behind your back—and tell you that is where you should hide money if you want to keep it safe. Randy, you would have never known he made the switch. That is why the scam is called "The Jamaican Switch." You would think that you had all the money and the second guy would find some reason for taking the first around that corner and as they say, "you would be left holding the bag."

"Come on," John said, opening the door to the bank. I have some business to take care of and you can put your money away."

John was going to ask how much Randy had in his hand but decided not to make him any more embarrassed than he seemed to be.

"How do you know all about this stuff" Randy asked sheepishly.

John going back into his crime reporter fiction said, "Well I once wrote something on it." John answered and smiled at his own private joke. What he had written on it was a criminal complaint when he worked for the DA's office.

"God damn! God damn! It's a good thing I ran into you! Here I was figuring that I finally got my paycheck in time to make it to the bank when all this happens to me."

John knew, whether he wanted him or not, he had just made a friend for life.

He didn't want Randy to see him changing all the bills so he just asked for change of one of his big bills.

When they were leaving the bank, Randy said, "I am just on my way to meet Harvey for a bite before I go back to work. Why don't you join us?"

John could not think of a reason not to. They left the bank and walked to a small restaurant. They sat at a table waiting for Harvey and Randy ordered beers for them.

Randy wanted to know what other things John had written about. John was in mood to tell old funny "war stories" so he decided to tell Randy about some of the lighter things his "lawyer friends had told him and that he had written about."

Randy said, "Well I guess if you write about crime and courts, you get friendly with a lot of lawyers."

John just smiled and related that one "lawyer friend had a client who had started out as burglar and moved on to become a fence. That's a person who buys stolen merchandise from a thief and sells to anyone looking for a real bargain and not too particular about why the price is so low. Because the lawyer represented the fence, he got a stream of thieves as clients.

"One of the thieves was a man name Shawn O'Sullivan. His specialty was taking a large set of pliers and twisting the locks out of doors. He was notorious for this MO—meaning *modus operandi* or to the non-Latin speaking police 'method of operation." Anyway, O'Sullivan specialized in business machines: Typewriters, calculators—that type of stuff. One night the police got a call that O'Sullivan was seen prowling near a building. While one set of officers tried to keep track of him another set went back to the place where he had been seen, and tried to find out if there had been burglary. The team at the scene could not find a place that had been burglarized, but the team following O'Sullivan got tired of him leading them around in circles so they stopped his car. When they stopped him, O'Sullivan demanded to know why they had stopped him. They said it was for suspicion of burglary. He said 'What burglary. I haven't hit any place in a week!" They made him open the trunk of his car. They said they were looking for business machines but all they found was a small box with some tools. They took the tools and took him to jail.

"They let him go after three days but kept the tools and put them through some tests. They found that the pliers left distinctive striation marks on the metal used for door locks. By matching the markings left by these pliers with the parts of the locks found at a burglary they were able to arrest him for the burglary from the last week."

"Can they do that?" ask Randy.

"They did it," John shrugged. "You have to realize what they were dealing with here. I mean this guy would tell the cops that they shouldn't hassle him because he wasn't working their district—as if that made him a citizen or something. Before they arrested him again after the tests, he had told them that since they had kept him in for three days, they were going to lose three machines. That night a place was burglarized and it had three typewriters and a calculator. One of the typewriters was left on the doormat. Guess who? So," John continued, "when you play those games, you have to expect lots and lots of heat."

"What other kind of stuff did this lawyer tell you about?" Randy asked, ordering two more beers.

"Wild stuff. He had a call one day from a guy that was helping rip off a house and was at the back door when he saw the police roll into the front yard. He started to go over a high wooden back fence but when he got his hands up on the top of it, and looked up, there was a huge black dog growling down from the other side. He kind of slunk down in the weeds hoping the cops wouldn't see him. One of them walked over and yelled 'You—what are you doing there?' This guy got up and brushed himself off and says "What does it look like I'm doing here. I'm trying to hide!"

John could not help but laugh at the story. The dog reminded him of another story. "I was in the lawyer's office one day when he got a call from a guy asking his advice for the caller's 'friend.' It seemed this 'friend' had burglarized a place and got away clean. The only problem was that his dog was locked inside the burglarized apartment."

When Harvey showed up, they spoke for a bit and John waved off the offer of another beer and said he had to get back to his writing. Randy said he understood.

John sat down in his living room thinking about his life on the coast. He missed some of it. He picked up some paper and thought about trying to write something but he couldn't. The beers had made him a little drowsy. It was late afternoon but he decided to take a nap.

He couldn't sleep. Then the idea for a story started.

He grabbed a pencil and paper. He chose a pen name and started to write.

"The Perfect Score" by John Stark

Just call me Vinny. That is all the name you need. Most people think that the perfect crime is when you do something to criminals 'cause they can't report it. Well, they're wrong. Like if you know where a guy hides his dope and you steal it from him. Well, he can't go to the police and say somebody took my dope. But the dope is only valuable if you can sell it to someone. The sale involves risk. You might sell it to an undercover nark. Which, by the way, a lot of my friends seem to have a real fondness for. That is the only way to explain it since they do it so often. Also, you could just get ripped off when you go to make the sale. No. That is not the way to go. But, the idea of taking from someone who could not go to the police is an important part of the puzzle. But, for it to be perfect, you need to get cash and you need to make sure that they never find out it was you that ripped them off.

Kidnapping! Kidnapping is the answer. But the big problem in kidnapping is handling the drop. How you get the money and no one knows it's you. It is when the kidnapper goes to pick up the money that he gets nailed.

In order to commit the perfect crime, you need a foolproof drop."

John was stuck. He didn't know a foolproof drop. He put the story down to think about it. He closed his eyes and tried to figure what would make a drop foolproof.

He had it.

There was that mountain in Placer County.

He and Marsha had taken a vacation up in the gold country. He saw a mountain that had a mine tunnel right through it. Alongside one end of the tunnel was a road that led up the mountain. From that end of the road, you could see the other side of the mountain where the other end of the tunnel was but you couldn't see the other end of the tunnel because it was hidden by some rocks and brush. The road that led to that hidden side of the tunnel was a long dead-end road that did not connect up with the road on the other side. John remembered the lay out and realized it was a perfect spot for a drop. It would be possible to hide on the mountain and watch the person bringing the money to the hidden side and make sure he was alone and not followed. Then go down the mountain and through the mine to get the money. From then it was simple to scamper back to where the car was and run like hell down the main road.

John wondered how he could get "Vinny" to explain the drop scenario so that it would make sense to a reader. He tried a couple of times but nothing worked. He just couldn't get his thoughts down on paper. He drifted off into thinking about the Placer area in California.

He wondered if he could ever go back and see it again. He wondered if his life would have been better if he had worked up there.

It was a rainy Monday. Steve and Dick were to set to meet Marsha at a restaurant to discuss what was happening with the insurance company. Steve had been handling all the arrangements for Marsha. His policy was with the same company, so it made sense. However, this plan was an area where Dick saw a potential conflict of interest for Steve and, even though Dick liked Steve, he was closer to John and felt he would hang around and keep an eye on Marsha's interests.

They had picked a time after the normal lunch hour so the restaurant would not be too crowded. Dick, who took a half-day vacation time from work, got there first and Steve showed up minutes later.

They knew they were going to have to wait for Marsha.

"You know Dick, no matter how crazy you thought my theory about what might have happened to John might have sounded, I'm starting to think I wasn't far off."

"I don't know, Steve what makes you think it's getting any better than when you first dreamed it up?"

"You know a guy named Nickie DelPesco?"

Dick leaned toward Steve and lowered his voice, "The ex-LAPD lieutenant, who the word is, went to work for the Frattini brothers? What's the story with that guy? I've never known a guy to retire as a cop and go to work for the wise guys."

"Yeah, that's him all right. You're right, it just goes to show how things can get turned around. In the old days, if the guys on the job heard from someplace like Chicago that Joe Spaghetti was flying into town, they would meet him at the airport and tell the guy not to step off the plane. If they missed him at the airport, one day real soon, when he was opening up his garage door or something, someone would come out of the bushes and hit him on the head with a sap. The guy would wake up with a note pinned to his chest that said, 'Go away!' or some other gentle hint."

Dick just shook his head. He had no doubt that that was how things used to be.

Steve continued, "But now, with all these courts coming down with all the damn rulings, it's too hard to do the damn job. And, with all this powder around, the money is just too damn big. That's the damn answer. The good side is too damn hard and the bad side is just too big. That's why a guy like DelPesco slides toward the other side.

"I started to get a hint the DelPesco was a dirty cop when we had a wire going with the Feds on a big drug operation. We found out from the wiretaps where the drug drop was. It was an old gas station on Sunset, near downtown. We were getting messages like 'Take two and put it in a bag and leave it at the place.'

"So, one night, after a call arranging a drop, DelPesco says he needs to take an hour to go meet a snitch of his. Next thing we know we are hearing calls, 'The stuff wasn't there, I'm no going to pay, blah blah blah.'

"And the other guy's yelling, 'You trying to rip us off, you got the stuff now you pay or else.' I mean these guys are going to go to war.

"Later on, we get enough evidence for a warrant and we take down a house we've been watching and taping.

There was a pile of powder in the back room. I mean they have scales and heat-sealing machines the whole works. When we go into the back room, there is a stack of bags of this white shit on a table.

"On another table, there are stacks of big bills. When we first hit the back room, I glanced at the table with the smack and it had several stacks of kilo bags. All the stacks looked like they had about the same height. But two looked like they were one bag higher than the others. You know, like two bricks sitting on a brick wall. Later, when we went to inventory the stuff, all the rows are even. I was sure it looked different but I didn't say anything.

"Well, when one of these dirt-bags cuts a deal and he starts talking about this and that. When he starts talking about what was in the place we took down, his numbers and our inventory don't match. We got two less bags of shit than this guy says was there, and we got 40 grand less in money. Now, DelPesco and I were the first guys in. I didn't have my eye on DelPesco the whole time so I can't be positive he took anything or where the hell he could have stashed it if he did. He and I did the inventory of what was in the stacks, and I know I didn't take anything.

"The head hunters from internal affairs came to me and asked how many kilos of the stuff I saw on the table and I told them what we inventoried was what we found. I wasn't going to go raise any suspicions in their minds. But, I sure as hell thought I saw more stuff when I went in than what came out in our boxes."

He looked at Dick, "Then I started thinking about that other night when DelPesco said he was going to go talk to his snitch and these guys are yelling that the stuff is missing from the gas station bath room. They didn't know we had them tapped. They weren't putting on a show for our benefit.

"To show you what I mean about the good side being so tough. We lost the case in court because the order for the wiretap was screwed up. And all these assholes, except the one that took the plea deal, just walked away from the whole thing. So, when you think of what the missing stuff was worth and what a cop gets paid you start to wonder why any cops are straight."

Steve could see Dick was squirming in his seat. He realized he could not tell Dick that one of the reasons he could not push DelPesco on the missing heroin was that when DelPesco was a sergeant, DelPesco had insisted a suspect Steve had just killed had had a gun. And DelPesco had been so sure, that when they couldn't find a gun, he supplied a gun himself.

Steve told Dick that DelPesco had come to his office supposedly just to shoot the breeze.

While he and DelPesco were talking about old times, he told Steve, "You and me go back all long way. I hear you may be pulling the plug on this bullshit and I'm happy for you. Just remember, I owe you one."

When Steve had said he thought they were even, DelPesco had insisted, "Not by my count. By my count I still owe."

"Anyway," Steve said, "When DelPesco showed up at the office yesterday, he said he was in the neighborhood and just wants to talk about old times. What he was talking about though is Snappy and John. Somehow, he got the information about that possible ID of John in the bar. He wasn't letting on why he was asking, but that was what he was dancing around. I figure if the road past Snappy was going to lead anywhere, maybe it was going to lead to the Frattini brothers. I think they want to make sure that the road is closed permanently. Someone is sure nervous, if they're gonna send a high stepper like DelPesco over to shoot the shit on a John and Snappy connection."

"What did you tell DelPesco?"

"What the hell could I tell him. As far as I know, John had nothing to do with Snappy. I mean I think he represented some of his people over the years. But I told DelPesco if he has any more questions about Snappy or what happened to John he should go and talk to Deputy District Attorney Richard Moran."

Steve smiled.

"When I mentioned your name, I could tell that he was going to run right over and talk to you," Steve laughed.

"Have you heard from him yet?"

Dick was not amused. Someone in the task force had to be giving even scraps of information, like the bar question, to people who should not have it. He didn't like it.

Steve saw Dick tense and his eyes narrow as Dick looked past Steve's shoulder.

"That didn't take long," Dick said under his breath.

Steve turned around and saw Marsha and Mathew walking into the restaurant holding hands.

Mathew stopped to check her coat. She came ahead to the table. She saw the look on their faces. All Marsha said as she sat down was, "I never like being alone."

Mathew came up and joined them at the table. After introductions, he sat next to Marsha but his chair was further back from the table than hers.

Steve told her about the insurance situation. They had just gotten a date to go to court. It was in six weeks. There would be papers for her to sign and he would let her know, as best he could, what was happening. Steve didn't anticipate any problems.

Steve held up his wine glass as if to propose a toast. He announced that as soon as the check cleared, he was retiring from the practice of law. He said he would have to work out with her how to split the money on a few cases.

He was going to look for some other lawyer to take over certain things and wind up some others.

"But," he said, "when that check clears, I am going on a trip. Pam has her eyes set on a new house and while they are painting it whatever color she decides on, we are going on a trip."

Marsha said, "I think that's great."

Dick said, "Marsha, you said you wanted to have a memorial service for John after the court decision. I assume, Steve, you could stay for that."

Marsha was nervous when he brought up the service. She looked back at Mathew. His nod told her that he had no problem with her burying the past.

Steve said defensively, "I'm sure we can work the timing out, Pam is making the actual travel plans. She is picking the places she wanted to go and the way she wants to get there. I don't care where it is or how long the trip takes. I am finally getting out of this rat race once and for all. Pam and I have wanted to be free of this business for a long time," he said slowly. "A real long, long time."

SIXTEEN

John woke up from his nap and wondered what to do for the rest of the night. He was angry with himself. Other than shopping, his trips to the bar and today's trip to the bank, his life seemed to have become centered around sleeping, eating ice cream and watching old movies. He was annoyed that he is letting himself get fat. He tried a couple of sit-ups. He got to five. Push-ups only three, and even then, he realized he was cheating.

The night was muggy. He got up and put his swim trunks on to go for a swim in the pool, but decided he didn't want the bother of getting all wet, then drying off and still smelling of chlorine even after a shower.

He took the money out of the tire and counted it. It was easy to count because he had put the money in banded stacks of $10,000 each. He counted fourteen stacks and fifteen lose hundred-dollar bills.

With nothing else to do John went to Lady's for a dinner. While sitting at the bar, Randy was just delivering John's hamburger platter when a sad old man, in the wrinkled suit, who Randy called "Professor" came in.

He had a milk-chocolate complexion with his white hair and sat on the stool next to John. Randy took his beer order and noted, as did John, that the small change coins used for payment did not amount to the cost of the beer. Without comment John slid a couple of coins from the change in front of him to make up the difference. The old man noticed and nodded to John.

In a thick accent, that John took to be Latin American, the Professor said, "Did you know the Greeks were practicing medicine and the Hippocratic Oath dates to five hundred years before the birth of our Lord?"

"No, I didn't."

John tried not to stare at the mangled hands the Professor used to try to hold his glass steady while he sipped. The Professor noticed John looking at his hands.

He put the glass on the bar and held them up. "You wouldn't believe it now, but I used to be a surgeon."

John knew there was more to come.

"One day our president of my homeland was visiting the University where I was a professor and the head of the surgery department. He was touring the hospital when an assassin shot him in the head. I had to push my way through the bodyguards to get to him. I immediately ordered them to take him to the surgery suite."

He paused, "I managed to save his life. At least for a while. There was great turmoil in the country. I was not political. All I wanted was to keep doing the job I loved. Taking care of patients and teaching students who would become doctors."

John nodded that he understood.

"Well, I say I saved his life for a while because the President was abducted from the hospital two days later and this time, they killed him." Then there was a coup. The military dictator took over and I was arrested for treason."

"For saving a man's life?"

"For saving *that* man's life."

John shook his head.

"After they arrested me, they broke my hands, wrists, and hit me so I was black and blue all over. They didn't ask me any questions. They knew I wasn't political and I had nothing I could tell them. They just did it because they could. One of them looked like he enjoyed doing it. I had nothing left there. They burned my house and barred me from teaching. After living on the street for years, my niece managed to bring me here with my broken hands and what was left of my mind. I had worked so hard for what I became in medicine."

Holding back a tear, he said, "They took it all away."

John could only shake his head, "I'm so sorry."

"For what?" He held up his hands, "You didn't do this to me."

John didn't know what else to say. The Professor went back to drinking his beer.

John listened but at times the Professor seemed to conflate stories from Greece, Egypt and Rome with his own life. No matter. John listened and paid for another beer. When the Professor was in mid-sentence, he excused himself and went to the men's room.

Randy came over and filled John in on more of what he was able to learn about the Professor. While they talked, two men with cowboy hats walked in and headed straight to the men's room. One of them acted as though there was urgency about his need to get there.

Randy cocked his head, "Are those boys lost? Is the rodeo in town?"

John chuckled.

Randy was resuming his talk when the door to the men's room flew open and the Professor landed on the floor outside the bathroom door.

They heard the yell, "This dirty old spick piece of shit shouldn't be allowed near a bathroom for decent people!"

John was walking over to tend to the Professor when the two strangers came out and stood over him. One kicked the fallen old man. As he approached, John could see the men look up at him. The kicking man made a fist and started toward John—then stopped. He backed up. He was looking behind John. John turned to see Randy gripping a baseball bat.

John went over to help the Professor up as he heard Randy say, "If you guys aren't out of my bar in five seconds this bat is going to smash some balls out of the park."

The two men looking at Randy—and the bat—were leaving, just as Lady burst in past them. She turned the big TV over the bar from a basketball game to an all-news channel saying, "I was listening to this damnedest thing in my car on the way over." She gave Randy a "what-did-I-miss?" look as he put the bat in its place behind the bar while John helped the Professor on the nearest stool.

The national news announcer proclaimed it was a live broadcast from Los Angeles. John eyed the news as he took the damp bar towel that Randy handed him for the Professor. The broadcast was from a news helicopter hovering over what looked and sounded like a war zone with dozens of flashing police car lights and the flashes and sounds of automatic weapon fire. Everyone in the bar was transfixed by the scene.

The news broadcaster recapped that LAPD, acting on a tip, was there in force, outside a warehouse in south LA getting ready to make a mass arrest of the notorious Mag 7 drug kingpins, when a rival group showed up evidently aiming to wipe the Mag 7 out. The police wound up in the middle of an automatic weapons battle.

This live coverage continued as John sat there watching the TV screen and as the Professor next to him put his head down on the bar and started to go to sleep mumbling about Greek and Egyptian medicine.

Lady with her eyes still on the news made a call.

In a few minutes, the Professor's niece came to gather him up and take him home, while the scene in LA, which was quickly dubbed "the Triangle Shootout," continued to play out.

John stared at the screen and wondered if those who killed Snappy could now be dead. He assumed it was not LAPD, but Snappy's killers could easily be on one of the other sides of the triangle.

He pondered what that could mean in terms of his freedom to go back to LA if he wanted to. He quizzed himself as to whether the idea—that he was fleeing some sort of personal danger— was not his own myth concocted to attempt to explain his disappearance if, for some reason, he was ever made visible again. Or maybe it was just his myth to tell himself why he jumped.

After the replays of the news from LA ended, and the basketball game was back on the big screen, John sat and looked around. He looked over in the corner and noted that the table that Tione usually occupied was still empty. He couldn't remember how many days it had been since he first noticed she was not there. He drank his last beer of the night and realized he missed seeing her.

Even after Randy's warning, there was something about the woman.

Lady noticed his look and as though reading his mind said, "Yeah. She hasn't been here this week. Randy is close to her—he says it's because they are both "sexual deviants.""

She chuckled and shook her head, "Anyway, he says she's with a steady who takes her to out of town and then she's retiring."

John was listening as Randy came up alongside Lady and said, "Yep. Tione is on a trip to London this week but when she comes back, Tione is retiring and Carla is going to be leaving town."

John felt sad at the news of her leaving. He recognized the sadness but he wasn't sure why. He liked to look at this woman but she had only said a few words to him—but still…

SEVENTEEN

Marsha watched the Triangle Shootout with a different concern. Mathew was at the game at the Forum, not far from where the shooting was taking place. She was hoping he was OK. In the month since she introduced Mathew to Dick and Steve, it was becoming more obvious to everybody that "Mat and Marsha" were a couple. Even though he had his own house, he preferred to move into hers. Especially when he found out that Marsha and John had the mortgage insurance that the bank made them take out as a condition of the loan so the bank would get all the money it lent, and the mortgage would be paid off, once John was declared dead.

Mathew moving in suited her fine, especially since he was getting more superstar attention. Josh Bonham the world-renowned star and the pinnacle of Hollywood celebrity in-group had been injured in a car crash in San Bernardino three weeks earlier. The emergency operation on his spine at the local hospital left him paralyzed from the waist down. Mathew was called in after Bonham was quickly transferred to an LA hospital.

The surgery he performed cleared the spinal canal. Bonham, for the first time since the accident, had feeling in his legs. He was expected to make a full recovery. The A-list celebrities who saw Mathew as the "Team Doctor" now wanted to invite him to events as "the Hollywood Doctor—our Doctor."

As Marsha went to the parties with him, she was enjoying her status. It was so obvious that he was smitten with her that Peter, after he had a little bit too much wine at a party, took her aside to counsel: "Two things you need to know about my brother. We were both altar boys, so it will mean a lot to our mom that you are a widow, not a divorcée, so you can be married in the church. He had been in a relationship with a divorced nurse he really liked a few years back, but when mom saw it was getting serious, she told him she would mourn him for dead if he didn't get married in the church."

Marsha just listened, wondering what Mathew had said to his brother that led to his talking about marriage.

He added, "And, while Mathew makes a ton of money, you might have noticed, he spends it as quick as he makes it—he almost had to go bankrupt once—so it's good that you will have that big check coming in."

Marsha didn't ask where he heard about the insurance payment but just smiled at him for his well-meaning advice.

Later in the week, Steve called and came over to talk about splitting fees on the cases John had handled and winding up the practice after the insurance money came in.

"Pam has decided she's in love with a house in the Hills and she is putting a down payment on it. This is assuming we can sell our place but the broker already has a couple lined up for our house. With the insurance money, we should be OK. I wish she liked a place that would not take so much of the million to close the circle between what the broker says our place will bring and the Hills place. But you know Pam. She wants what she wants."

Marsha nodded.

As Steve was leaving, he said. "I'll give you more details on the court thing and Pam asked if you want her help planning the memorial."

"Thanks Steve. I'll give Pam a call."

Alone after he left, Marsha sat and reflected on the changes in her life since John had disappeared.

EIGHTEEN

Home after the excitement with the Professor and the shootout, John again started thinking about the televised battle. Then his thoughts turned again to things from his career in LA. But this time was different. He realized a story was being born in his head piecing together tidbits of what he had done or heard. He grabbed a pad and started to write. Using the pen name—he had created for himself— he wrote:

"West LA One" by Jim Stark

It was one of those mornings when Mark could see the mountains. He headed north from the freeway up La Cienega Blvd. to the parole office. It had rained all day Sunday, and as the say, the rain had washed away the smog.

Mark Berg, a Parole Agent for the California Department of Corrections, had made this trip to the West Los Angeles Parole Unit One almost every Monday morning for the two years he had been in California.

On the mornings like this, that were clear and bright, he couldn't wait to get into the field; making home calls, checking on his parolees.

He parked his state issued Dodge in the parking lot of a bright new shopping mall, and took the escalator to the second floor. He turned away from the glittering department stores and headed down the dingy corridor to where the West LA office was tucked away.

He was just moving a little metallic doughnut marker from "OUT" to "IN" when he heard his boss's voice.

"Boy, did you have a busy weekend!" Mark waited until his middle-aged boss, looking slightly less rumpled than usual, emerged from behind the row of file cabinets.

"I'm going to assume that you don't have our apartment bugged, so you must be talking about work. I'll bite. How busy was I?"

"You no doubt heard that your man, Jordan Williamson, was shot on Friday. Well, SSU arrested another one of your men, Danny Perino, on Saturday. They figure him for the shooting. An old beef from Folsom. They were there at the same time."

"Yeah, I heard about Jordan, I called but no hospital would own up to having him. This Perino thing is a pain. I hope these guys didn't let the publicity spook them into making a mistake. It took me almost all of last week to line up a job for Perino. If he sticks to it, in six months he'll be making more than me."

"Well, right now he's in central jail. Jordan's in Queen of Angels. The booking numbers and the hospital room number are in SSU's emergency report on your desk. Looks like you got the shooter and the shootee! Have a good time!"

Mark got to his desk, checked the report and called his wife. They had an appointment to meet for lunch and then go to the doctor's office. They were expecting their first child in about three months.

"Hi, sweets. Look, I can't make it this afternoon. This thing about Jordan getting shot has really hit the fan. The Special Services Unit, the guys how handle special cases in the department, locked up one of my other guys. This Perino I told you about.

"I had heard that SSU had an interest in Jordan since he became the director of Harambe House. They figure Perino as a member of the Aryan Brotherhood. It's a group of wannabe Nazi cons. There had always been rumors that the Brotherhood was out to get Jordan either for some crap up at Folsom or they just don't like guys who run Black self-help groups. Besides, the more guys Jordan gets to clean up, the fewer customers the dealers have. Anyhow, since Perino just got out two weeks ago and now this…Well, I've got to go and find out.

"It looks like I'll be tied up with this all day. I want to see Jordan and I have to see Perino. I'll probably stop by the print shop where I got Perino that job just so I don't blow the connection. I might need it again for someone else.

"Good luck with the doctor. Sorry about the lunch, sweets. Maybe later in the week, OK?"

He called the hospital. Williamson said he was feeling better. He hadn't seen who shot him. Mark told Jordan about Perino and the Brotherhood. Jordan said he didn't know if the shooting had been "related to the joint of not." There was something in the way he said that though. Mark thought Jordan was hedging a little. Jordan said he had an idea about the shooting but didn't want to discuss it over the telephone. Mark told him he'd be up to see him after his jail visit.

Mark headed for the door and moved his doughnut. "Put me out to the jail and the hospital," he called to the secretary. "I wanted to be out in the field today anyway. If anyone from SSU calls tell them to play with someone else's case load. These guys are mine."

The jail visit came first. It took twenty minutes from the time Mark put in the request until they brought Perino down. Around the fifteenth minute, Mark hoped they had not already shipped him to one of the outlying facilities. Mark had played that game before. It seemed to him that just when he was about to give up hope, and resign himself to the fifty-mile trip to the Honor Ranch, that his man would appear.

He could see Perino was agitated when he arrived. "Hey man, you got to get me out of here. I didn't do this! Why'd they grab me? It wasn't even cops. It was parole guys. Why'd you let them do this. I was getting it together. I don't know anything about this."

"Slow down!" Mark interrupted. "I didn't let anybody do anything. They don't need my approval to do anything. The report says they busted you because they heard the Brotherhood had a contract out on Williamson. The wire from the joint says that you're in the Brotherhood. Also, you wouldn't tell them where you were at the time of the shooting."

"I didn't tell them where I was because they didn't ask. They just told me the guy was shot and they figured me for it."

"They didn't ask where you were at the time of the shooting?"

"Well, not exactly. See, they rolled up on me and said, 'Have you gone anywhere today?' and I said 'No.' One of them, a big guy, looks like an Indian, said, 'He's lying.' and they took me."

"Were you lying?"

"Yeah."

"Wonderful! Now you want to tell me the story?"

"I ain't gonna talk about the joint or being in any Brotherhood while I was there. But I see in the paper in here that Williamson was shot about two thirty near that place of his. I was nowhere near there. Right about then I was in an accident on Sunset near Doheny. It was a fender bender but there should be some broken glass still there."

"And you didn't tell them about it because…" Mark said, with an intonation that told Perino to fill in the blank.

"Because after you got me the job, I went out and bought an old car so I could get to work. I bought it before I got your permission. And, I was driving it without a license when I tapped another car in the rear. Look, it's the God's honest truth. I was going to tell you about the car today, and ask you to help me get my license. You've got to help me get out of here. I'm going nuts. Look, the car is at my mom's place. Please, just go over there and you can see the broken headlight. It broke when I tapped the other guy in the rear. I didn't want no trouble, so I gave him the fifty he wanted—the crook! Fifty bucks for bullshit I had all the damage all he had was a small dent in the chrome and a small crack in the taillight. Anyhow, I gave him the money and he took off. No cops, no nothing. I don't think he could have stood the heat either, if you know what I mean. So just check the car and check the scene. You'll find my glass and a tiny piece of his tail light. It would be the south side of the street, about fifty feet from the corner."

"Danny, you know it rained yesterday."

"Oh, man, it didn't rain that hard. You gotta go check. Please? I gotta get out of here and ah… I don't want to lose that job.

"OK. I'll check. I don't know how much good it will do. I'll be in touch."

"Please man, fast?"

"OK. OK. I'm going, I'm going."

Mark looked into his field book. Under the mug shot of Perino on the fact sheet he found his mother's address. Sure enough, there was a car with a broken headlight on the grass. Mark looked around but no one was there. He took a piece of the broken glass, looked at it, and shaking his head, put it in his pocket. He thought, "Well, now you're a crime lab. Oh well, you promised."

He drove to the corner of Doheny and Sunset. It was on what is called "The Strip." As he parked his car and began looking for glass, what he saw was water. A wide track of water. He noticed there were no cars. He looked up at the sign. "No parking/Monday 8AM to 11AM/ Street Cleaning."

"Wonderful. This poor guy has a lot of luck. But, it's all bad. If the rain don't get him then the sweeper will!" He threw the fragment into the trash barrel. "Oh well, so much for glass. But, as long as I'm here, I wonder if anybody saw the accident."

He looked around. There was a bank across the street with a drive-up window. He walked up.

"Excuse me Miss." I wonder if you could help me. Did you see an accident here on Friday afternoon? It would have been across the street."

"I'm sorry. I was on vacation. I just got back today."

"Do you know who was here? It would have been about 2:30."

"Yes, that would be Linda. But she just went on vacation. She'll be back in two weeks."

He asked, "Do you know of anyone who might have seen the accident?"

Then he had an idea. "Do you stamp the time of day on the transactions? Maybe someone could look at Friday's records and see if anyone was here doing business around that…"

He stopped in mid-sentence. Out of the corner of his eye he saw a camera with a red light. He looked over to the teller's right and he saw a TV screen. It was a monitor of a closed-circuit TV system. The camera was aimed so he could see himself. But he could also see the street behind him.

"Miss, who can I see about getting a look at the tapes?" he said as he pulled his badge out of his pocket. "I'm a Parole Agent and it's very important."

The bank manager sent him to an office in the back of the bank. He identified himself to a Mr. Johnson, the head of security. Mark explained what he wanted. Mr. Johnson, a retired policeman, said it would take a few minutes.

While he was setting up the tape, the neatly dressed security chief smiled. "I don't live but a few blocks from Harambe House. The word I hear is the Mr. Williamson was shot by some lady's husband."

The tape was now playing. After a short while, Mr. Johnson pointed. "Is that your man over there?"

"Yes, that's him. The one with the wallet open and no driver's license in it."

Mark grinned, "Thanks a lot. I know one parolee who is going to be very happy. Can I use your telephone?"

Mark called his office and explained how he had spent the morning. His boss agreed to drop the "parole hold" that was keeping Perino in jail. Mark told his boss he would swing by the hospital on the way back to the jail.

At the door to Jordan's room, Mark encountered two very large Black men. They each had on black pants, a black sweatshirt, and a black beret. Over the left breast on the sweatshirts was the word "Harambe." Each man had a beard and was wearing dark glasses.

They stepped in front of him, "Who are you, man!"

"Gentlemen. I'm his man." Mark smiled. "Now, move out of my way. Hey Jordan. How are you doing?" he said pushing past them into the room.

"I'll make it."

He told Jordan of his detective work. Jordan just frowned.

Mark said, "OK. So, I figured out who didn't shoot you. Now if you'd like to tell me who you think did—I'm told the word on the street is irate husband."

Jordan smiled. He and Mark had arrived at the West LA unit at about the same time. Jordan from Folsom, and Mark from a job with a drug program in New York.

Jordan started slowly, "Look, I still don't know for sure. If the community sees it as 'irate husband' that's OK with me."

"But…" Mark said leaving the blank.

Jordan cleared his throat. "But I saw my girlfriend Doreen's car across from where I got hit. She and I had a little discussion earlier that morning and she ain't been to see me. So…"

"So, you knew it wasn't Perino when we spoke this morning."

"Look, I said, ain't sure. I didn't see anybody do it. So, if someone tags Perino that's OK too."

"Well, it's not OK for me Jordan. I put a lot of work into this guy."

"Look Mark. We've been around a bit. And I think you're OK. But as far as I'm concerned you can leave that Aryan 'Bothered-hood' right where he is."

Mark shook his head. "Sorry Jordan, I'm on my way to make sure he's cut loose right now. By the way, where were those two body guards of yours when you got hit?"

"I don't know, but under the circumstances… Anyway, they sure are attentive now," he laughed

Mark laughed too. "OK, your secrets safe with 'old closed mouth.' Stay out of trouble, will you? Catch you latter."

"Hey wait a minute," Jordan called, "How's the baby coming, Mark?"

"A few months to go."

"You gonna name it after me?" Jordan grinned.

"Only if it's black, Jordan. Only if it's black."

As Mark walked out of the room, he could hear Jordan's chuckle, "Cold! My man is so cold!"

By the time Mark got to the jail, Perino was just having his property returned to him.

"Oh, you're beautiful! You found the glass, huh?"

"It's a long story, Danny. I'll tell you on the way home. Let's just say that this is the first time on record that a bank camera got somebody out of this place."

Mark stopped. He put his hands on Perino's shoulders. "Danny, ah, I hate to bring this up at a time like this, but ah—you want to run me that bit again about the car and the driving without a license?"

When John had finished his story, it was almost daylight. He was tired but elated. He had finally written something. He repeated, "only if it's black" out loud. He laughed. He loved the line.

He realized he had not heard himself laugh in a long time. He thought about the scenes in the story that he had adapted from his life. They were not all really bad times. There had been good times.

John was starting to get sad that he had would never have them again.

Then he started to think though the implications of being a writer. So, the pen name would be fine. But just how far could he take it. If he started to get well known as a writer would have to wear a disguise? Maybe have to have plastic surgery? Could he go back to his old haunts as a new person?

He decided that he didn't have to decide anything right now. He was thinking about how he missed some of the LA places when he fell asleep.

NINETEEN

When John woke up, he didn't want to get out of bed. He felt sad, but could not remember why. He thought about last night. He was happy to have written something but he thought his sadness was caused because he had not figured out what to do about fame as a writer. He laughed and told himself he would cross the bridge if he ever came to it. Then he thought about the news of Carla leaving. Could that be it? How could it? She had only spoken a couple of words to him but yet he was in-trigued—and he was attracted by her. He thought, The whole Carla-Tione thing is curious.

He put thinking of her aside and tried to figure out how to spend this day. Since he had found the apartment, he had not been more than a few blocks away from it. He thought his whole stay so far could be characterized: OK. So, I'm here—now what? He decided that he would drive around the Miami area and discover places he hadn't bothered to find during his insular stay in the area.

When he started driving, he had no destination in mind other than to see water. If a light turned red, he could decide to wait for it to turn green or make a right turn. He ended the drive, as he knew he would, back at Lady's lounge.

Randy saw him come in, "OK. John what will it be?" He moved his hand above his head, "Are you up to here with the burger platter, and ready to try something else?"

John shook his head, "Nope, the usual burger platter if you please."

Randy said, "Well at least I know tomorrow will be a different experience for you."

'Oh, yeah?"

"Yep. Tomorrow you are going ice skating in the afternoon."

"Nah, I don't think so, I haven't been on skates since I was a kid, and sure as hell don't want to break my ass on the ice."

He chuckled, "Although I did have a paramedic friend who used to say, 'If you fall down and break something on ice, at least you already got the injury iced down.'"

Randy shook his head at the bad joke, "I never heard that one. But I know you're coming."

"Why are you so sure?"

"Carla's coming. She called this morning. She's back in town. She had asked me to teach her how to ice-skate. She made me promise to invite you."

He shrugged, "Hey, frankly I don't think you're all that much, but just because we are both sexual deviants, it doesn't allow me to understand the working of the lesbian mind."

Randy smiled as he pushed a piece of paper into John's shirt pocket with the address of the ice rink and the time to be there and smiled, "So now you're invited— you'll be there."

John sat at the bar for the rest of the night. He had his few beers and refrained from grilling Randy about anything else Carla had said about him.

John went back to his apartment wondering about tomorrow.

At three the next afternoon, John showed up at the rink. Randy and Harvey were there. No Carla.

Randy saw the look on John's face. "Don't worry," he chuckled, "if she says she'll be here, she'll be here."

Carla showed up, with a knit hat and matching sweater with tight fitting jeans, and hugged Randy and Harvey.

She smiled at John. "In three weeks, I'm moving to Sault St. Marie, Michigan. I bought a pair of skates."

She held them up for John to see, "I figured I've earned the right to spend my remaining Miami time doing whatever I'd like to do."

She sat and laced up her skates. "Right now, I want to learn to skate."

John watched as Randy and Harvey each took Carla by an arm and guided her onto the ice. She learned and got her balance very quickly. When the free skating period was over and music started to play. Randy and Harvey took off and whirled around together. Carla reached out for John. He took her arm and they moved slowly around the edge of the ice, staying close to the boards so as not to get run over by the pirouetting dancing couples.

Carla said, "You're doing very well."

"I learned as a kid. I can't remember the last time I did this though."

"Well, I guess it's one of those things you don't forget. By the way, are you watching the movie of the week tonight?"

John hadn't given it much thought but he said. "I guess I can. Why?"

"Well Randy says Lady always has to watch the awards on the big TV at the bar. I'm only interested to know if Jodi Worren wins, but I can find that out tomorrow. I'd much rather watch the movie about that case in

California. I don't have a TV. Would you mind if I came over and watched with you?"

They both knew he wasn't going to refuse, but she added, "I'll bring a pizza and a bottle of wine."

"What kind of wine?" John asked as though that was the deciding factor.

She laughed and said, "You can have anything you want," in a seductively playful way that had nothing to do with white, red, or rosé.

When they were leaving the rink, Randy asked if he would see John later for his usual dinner order. John smiled and said he had a better offer—he had to stay home and watch TV and eat pizza. Randy looked at Carla.

She just grinned.

Carla, knocked on John's door just before the movie was starting. Now her straight black hair was down to her shoulders. John noticed she was bare foot and wearing faded cut-off blue jeans that were cut so short that John could see half of the front pockets dangling down. She wore a short sleeve blue work shirt tied in a knot between her breasts. John noticed she had a net bag dangling from her wrist that held two bottles of wine and something he could not make out. She pushed the box of pizza toward him. He took it from her, and looked to clear a place to put it, as she looked for a place to put down the two bottles of wine.

As she placed the bottles on the only clear spot on the table, she chuckled, "Do you at least have plates?" She headed for the kitchen alcove where she found the few things she needed in the cabinets. John cleared the papers off the rest of the small Formica table and pulled up the two of the three chairs that came with it. Beside the chairs, all he had to sit on facing the TV was a big wicker seat and an old wooden milk box. They both realized that no matter how long John had been there, she was his first visitor.

She looked at the bare walls. "How long have you been here?" Before John could answer she said, "I mean I don't see any pictures on the wall. It looks like you got here yesterday."

"Well, it's been longer than that, I guess I'm not a picture kind of guy."

She smiled, "What flavor wine to do you want, we have white or red, or should I mix them together to make rosé?"

John knew she was kidding about flavors and how to make rosé, "From what I've seen you're the wine drinker."

Groaning, she said, like she was talking to a child, "Should I have brought you a six-pack?"

He laughed, "Nope. I'll try to eat like a grownup. Red will be fine."

As they ate, they turned to watched the movie. Watching TV with Carla in the room became a very different experience. John had a hard time taking his eyes off her. She piled her hair high on her head with her hand to get it off her neck for a moment before she let it drop as she took a drink of her wine. He watched her bare legs fold under her and then unfold as she tried to get comfortable in the big wicker seat. He started to say he was sorry that the seat was so uncomfortable but decided not to say anything. After all, it was the only seat he had.

When they chatted during the commercials, John tried hard not to show that he was getting homesick watching the movie. He recognized the streets where the movie was shot. He recognized the courthouse where he had spent so much of his time. The office they used for the fictitious lawyer was the office of a real lawyer who John knew well. In fact, John had been in that office two weeks before he left LA.

Watching the movie, John saw one familiar place after another. In one of the courtroom scenes John recognized the woman who played the court reporter. She actually was a court reporter and had told John years earlier that her boyfriend in "the business" would occasionally get her jobs. John started to grow sad as he reflected on never seeing these people and places again.

He started to wonder if he had made a mistake and how he could undo to it if he wanted to.

In one courtroom scene, John kept his mouth shut but found it hard not to point out the mistakes in evidence and procedure. He winced as one of the lawyers walked into the well of court straight up to the front of the judge's bench to make a point.

Carla saw John's reaction but made no comment.

Instead, she asked, "Who do you think did it?"

"I have no idea at this point," John said. He really didn't. While, the show was said to be a dramatization of a real case, the facts seemed a bit different from the case John knew about, and he was only partially familiar with the real case. Also, distracted by Carla, he was having some difficulty following the twists in the plot.

The show started again and they watched in silence. John smiled and shook his head as one scene started with a view of Marina Del Rey. John thought that was terribly ironic. He looked to see if he could see Dick's boat. He thought that would make the night complete. The movie ended with a chase scene with one of the villains ending up getting shot and falling into the water at the Marina. John remembered now, that in the real case, there had been a shooting and the body wound up in one of the Venice canals not in the Marina.

After the movie, he was wondering what to do next. She said, "Randy told me you had been in LA as crime reporter."

He nodded.

"Was this a case you covered?"

"No. Even through it's set in modern LA, the real case actually unfolded before my time."

"What did you do before you were a crime reporter?"

He smiled, "Well for a long while I was a child."

She laughed. "I hardly remember being a child. But, remember I spent a good part of my childhood in court-rooms like that."

John was wondering if she had been a juvenile delinquent.

She caught the look in his eye and realized what he was thinking.

"No. I was not a juvenile delinquent, I saved that for when I was a grownup." She chuckled. "No. My mother was a court clerk. Luckily, she worked for an older woman judge who understood that my single-parent mom would occasionally have to bring her only-child daughter with her to work when there was no school or other places for me to be. The judge told mom that she would rather have me sitting in the back of the courtroom than have to deal with a temp clerk. She'd relegate me to her chambers, like her office, if the kind of case she was hearing was one I shouldn't see."

John nodded.

She shook her head, "More than once I heard my mom's judge say, 'When I was raising my kids, I used to wonder how any working mother ever gets to go to work—she has to be well, her kids have to be well, the sitter needs to be well, and the sitter's kids need to be well.'

"I never thought of that."

She looked at the TV and asked, "Can we turn that off?"

John could read the implication that she had something serious to talk about.

He turned the set off. Poured them both another glass of wine and sat facing her.

She started, "Look you know about Tione. It was my business. If my guys had a wife I was never going to talk to the wife and if they didn't have a wife, they knew I wasn't looking to become their wife. It was as uncomplicated as I could make it. Sometimes it was hard work spending my time telling men what they wanted to hear

"Men don't want to deal with the courtship ritual and both men and women like uncomplicated sex.

"Now, Tione has made more than enough to retire in style. I'll never have to work again. I'm only going to be here three more weeks."

She paused, "After that I'm heading up to Sault St. Marie to be with Jeanna and have my baby."

The mention of "her baby" surprised him and she could see it.

"Yeah. I know." She continued, "Jeanna and I decided we wanted children and I wanted to get pregnant." Jeanna is finishing her tour of duty in the Navy and has a job lined up on a Great Lakes cargo ship. We met when we started at the Naval Academy."

"You went to Annapolis?"

"Yeah, I was an Air Force brat for my first 9 years. And, we were all over the world. I speak several languages. My dad was always absent from the home but mom followed him. When he died, we moved back to the states and she got the court clerk job. I'm not sure why I choose Navy over the Air Force academy except I was close to my high school coach who had a brother that played for Annapolis and Coach said he would make the call if I wanted. So, I just went with it. It's funny how things just happen.

"I was the goalie on the varsity soccer team. But I tore up my knee in my second year and I got a medical discharge. By then Jeanna and I were a couple and I decided to stay in Annapolis so we could be with each other when we could."

She looked to see if he was following, and trying to fit the pieces together. She chuckled, thinking a little more history was in order. "OK. So, I went to a junior high school where there were ten girls for every boy. All the girls wanted to be popular and be the one with the boyfriend. The guys expected the girls to put out. I realized early on that I was more attracted to the girls in our bullshit sessions than I was to the guys, but I wanted very badly to fit in. The girls thought of giving head as a way to have a boyfriend and keep your virginity."

She looked as John. "I know. I know. But, while I was becoming aware of my interest in girls, I was also becoming aware that I liked giving blow jobs. I liked the feel in my mouth, but I really really liked the feeling of power. Sometimes I'd get off on it."

She looked at him and continued, "Hey. I realized that I can like the feeling of a horse between my legs as I'm riding, but that doesn't mean I'm sexually attracted to horses, any more than liking to drive makes me attracted to cars. By the time I got the Academy and met Jeanna I knew for sure who I was. So, after I tore up my knee, I was wondering how I was going to support myself while I stayed close to her. I mean there weren't a lot of jobs for gimpy goalies."

He smiled.

"I saw an ad for a live-in caregiver. A woman was looking for someone to live in and help take care of her crippled son. One night, when I had been there a couple of weeks, after I put him to bed, she delicately brought up the subject of his sexual needs. She said she had a girl who used to come in but she had died of an overdose and she was wondering…"

John started to nod his head as he realized where this was leading.

"When Jeanna graduated and was stationed out of Okinawa, there was no need to stay in Annapolis, so I moved here and Tione was born. First, I worked for a friend of the woman whose kid I started with. My new boss had a theory that Florida cops were too cheap to fly their guys out of town so they could land at the airport and look like tourists. So, she screened guys and would only send us with those who she knew or could prove they had flown into town. That kept us out of legal hassles and the guys who drove us stayed outside—that kept us safe. By the time she decided to get out of the business, I already had some regulars."

She anticipated his question. "Yes. Jeanna knows what Tione did for a living, but she says she won't object as long as it ends when we get back together."

She chuckled, "She says as long as it's not another woman she can't object to me making love while she's making war. As you may have noticed, Tione has some very exclusive high-end clients. It was the total girlfriend experience—with guys who don't want the entanglement of a full-time girlfriend. Sometimes there was no sex at all. When there was, usually the sex is all head and very little actual straight or vaginal. I don't like vaginal all that much and I have the power to choose who I'm with, so I could pretty much get to do as I pleased. Like that African prince you saw me with the other night. His father runs the oil export business for his country. There are not enough pain pills on the planet for me to let him put his python in my pussy. But when I got through with what he was thinking was just foreplay, he wasn't able to do anything I didn't want."

John chuckled and she smiled at her turn of phrase. "But my guy who took me to England, we went two months back—he's gorgeous with a scale topping income and way above the charts IQ. I know he's not all that big and it was the right time of the month for me—he has great genes—so Jeanna and I agreed it would be an OK time for me to get pregnant. He doesn't know and never will."

She looked at John and studied him for a second. "So, here's the deal."

He leaned forward.

"I have only a short time to be here now, and there are things I have never seen here. Would you believe I haven't gone to the beach or the zoo or down to the Keys? So, I'm looking for a short-term boyfriend experience. Randy told me he thinks you're a good guy and he told me about how you got him out of jam at the bank and how you looked out for the Professor. He's got Harvey and not much time. Have you been to the zoo yet?"

John shook his head. "Truthfully, I haven't but with what I think you're offering I'd be tempted to lie even if I had."

"Just as long as you know the limits, I don't want any weakness when it's time to say goodbye."

He nodded, "No weakness. No whining!"

"Good."

She got the net bag that she brought the wine in and took out what looked like a handful of string.

"I need a man's opinion. This is a bathing suit I just bought. Tell me what you think."

"Think about what?"

"The suit silly," she laughed.

"What suit? All I see is a handful of string."

"I have to put it on to give you a better idea." She smiled. "By the way am I keeping you up?"

John looked down at his pants. He smiled sheepishly and said, "Not yet."

Carla chuckled.

She turned around and untied the knot it her shirt. With her back turned, she took the shirt off and put on the new top. She reached around and tried to tie it. "Can you get that for me?"

He tied a bow and she turned around.

John could see the crochet top just covered her nipples.

"If you're going to wear that to a beach, I'm gonna need a shotgun to protect you."

She pushed him back down into his chair. She reached into the bag and took out what he knew must be the bottom. He waited to see what was going to happen next. He knew that turning her back while putting this on was not quite the same as putting on the top. He didn't have to wait long. She stepped back and pulled down her shorts. She watched John's face as she stepped out of the cutoffs and started to pull up the bottom of the suit. When she pulled it up, she made a show of modeling for him.

She asked, "Do you like?"

"Yes. And the suit looks good too."

She took his hand and guided him to his feet. She put her arms around his neck and kissed him. While keeping one arm around his neck, she slid her other hand down his pants.

He started to get hard at her touch. "Am I keeping you up?"

"Yes, and I like it."

She said, "Very nice," and pulled his pants down to his knees. She was still holding him in her hand as she started walking to the bedroom. John stopped for a second to step out of his pants so he wouldn't feel like an idiot hopping after her.

When she got to the bedroom, she laughed at the size of the bed. It took up nearly the whole room. Still holding onto him, she steered him backwards onto the bed.

She reached behind and untied the bow and let the top slide down her arms and off. She positioned herself between his legs. She gave him a big smile before she leaned down and took him in her mouth.

With his head on the pillows, John could see and feel what she was doing with her mouth. He watched as she seemed to get excited by it.

He closed his eyes to concentrate on his own sensations. He opened them again to watch and feel her tongue complete a circle around the head his penis before she went down and took it fully into her mouth. He felt his body tighten. He knew that if she did that a few more times he would explode.

It didn't take a few.

He groaned as he felt like his whole body was bursting through his penis—like he had just been turned inside-out.

She stopped and held him as he softened in her hand. She smiled at him.

After a few moments when he felt he could talk, he shook his head and said, "I lost my virginity twenty years ago and I've never had an orgasm before."

She cocked her head in disbelief, "You've never had an orgasm before."

"Oh. Sure, I thought I had had orgasms before but. . ."

He shook his head. "And now I have this. The greatest orgasm in the western hemisphere and from a pregnant lesbian."

She chuckled and rolled up to lie alongside him.

She asked, "OK. Boyfriend, what do you want to do tomorrow?"

"More. I sure as hell hope."

She laughed. "Yeah, I know, but I mean the zoo or the beach."

"Let's see what the weather looks like in the morning. OK? I think they are predicting a storm."

"OK. We'll see what the winds will let us tourists do. I'll call you in the morning."

After she left, John thought, Wow! Who wouda thunk that?

When he could take his mind off Carla—or maybe it was Tione? —his mind slipped back to the movie.

He tried to remember the name of the court reporter. Was it Carol or was she named Carla too? He fell asleep with his mind wandering around the LA streets he had just revisited on the TV.

TWENTY

John and Carla spent every day of the next week going to the beach or to other places that Carla said she wanted to go. John went along with all her suggestions. Pretending they were an old married couple, when she would tell him what she wanted to do, he would just say, "Yes, dear."

Carla's mouth and hands lived up to her end of their bargain.

John had to remind himself that he had signed up for a time limited deal. He needed to steel himself from fantasizing a future she had so clearly told him would not exist. When Carla and John would show up at Lady's, Randy would smile knowing what their arrangement was and glad to see that two people he considered friends were enjoying time together.

One night as they sat at the bar watching a crime drama that was set in New York City, John groaned when he heard the police in the radio car being sent to a "211" in progress.

When Carla asked him what was wrong, he said, "I just hate lazy screen writing."

She cocked her head and waited for him to finish.

"211 is the California Penal Code section for Robbery. Rather than take the few minutes it would be to find out what it would be New York, they just write what they think they know."

Carla said, "Well there aren't that many people here that that would bother, but. . ."

The next day, Carla had to run errands regarding getting some of her stuff shipped and getting her car ready for her trip. She and John had a plan to meet the next day.

That night, John had a thought. It was late and he didn't want to be alone. He thought Carla should be home from her errands.

He was lying in bed and thinking about what she did with him. He picked up the phone.

When he heard her voice he said in a matter-of-fact tone, "Is this room service? I would like to order a blow job. I would like it with all the trimmings and I would like you to deliver it now."

He heard her giggle and say it was coming right up.

He hung up.

He unlocked his door, turned out all the lights, got into his bed and waited.

After a while he started to worry if he had dialed the wrong number. It had sounded like Carla's voice, but perhaps it was someone else. All she had said was that it was coming right up.

She only lived a few blocks away, but that didn't mean that it was really Carla or that she knew it was John. He started to wonder if he had called some strange woman, who she would think the caller had been. He started to speculate on who the woman might be and what her reaction might be. He wondered if somewhere some guy was about to get a blow job. Were there many women who would respond to a call like that?

He started to reassure himself that he had recognized Carla's voice but as he waited, he wondered if he had misjudged Carla.

Maybe she wouldn't respond to such a request. He wondered why he thought he could get away with such a move. Maybe she did not recognize his voice. He resisted the temptation to go into the living room and call again.

As he waited still longer his thoughts turned to who she might have thought it was if it wasn't him. Who else she might deliver his order to.

Just then John heard Carla let herself in. He took a deep breath and tried to relax.

When she finished, John was pleased with himself for taking the risk and making the call. Then she asked if he minded if she spent the night. With a lot of her stuff shipped, she didn't feel like her place was "home" any more.

He smiled in the dark and said, "Yes, dear."

The next night when they went to the bar. Lady asked if she could speak to John. She didn't mind if Carla overheard or not.

Lady explained. She had to go see a lawyer for her daughter and wanted John to go with her. She thought with his background as crime reporter he probably had a lot of experience around lawyers, also because of her personal history with this lawyer, she didn't want to see him alone.

She told them she had not seen her daughter, Gail, for a long time. They had a disagreement about the company Gail was keeping. Gail had been arrested for drug possession three years ago and was given a prison sentence that was suspended and she was placed on probation. She did well on probation and her probation was due to expire when she was arrested. Now, the term of probation was suspended so that it would not expire before the new arrest was resolved. There was going to be a probation revocation hearing in Ft. Lauderdale. If the arrest meant she had violated her probation she would start the long term in prison.

Carla winced and put her arm around Lady's shoulder as John asked what she knew about the circumstance of the arrest. John wondered what facts were being left out, but thought from what Lady was able tell him, the case against Gail might not stand up.

Lady then told him in the past she had dated the lawyer but dumped him before giving him what he clearly wanted. He had become a very prominent attorney who let it be known that he could get people out from under some very serious situations.

She was upset. She told them that when she spoke to the lawyer about coming to see him about her daughter's case, he told her she should come in for a consultation and he intimated that if they went forward that he wanted sex to be part of their deal. He told her his usual fee was 15 thousand dollars but he might cut it in half as his discount fee.

John could not believe that some attorney would be so bold and open in a clearly unethical matter. He understood why Lady wanted someone to go with her. She also wanted to see if John felt the lawyer was right for the case and to find out more about what the police said they had, since she did not know if she could trust Gail's version when she told her she had nothing to do with what happened.

John was intrigued about the attorney. He wondered what a big-time Florida lawyer's office looked like. With Carla showing obvious concern for Lady's situation, he decided to go.

They entered an ornate office with lots of photos of the lawyer and political types. His name was Limogi Gigganti. He dressed in a flashy suit and had a couple of very ornate rings. He was six-four with coke bottle glasses and slicked back thick black hair. He had thick lips and an oversized smile. Sometime people riffing on first name called him "Oh Gee," making a bending back exaggerated fright expression.

He was clearly annoyed that Lady had brought someone with her.

As John listened to the interview the talk reminded him of what he came to dislike in Steve—the idea that practicing law was a volume business. In fact, seeing Oh Gee and listening to his rap, made John more aware of his dislike being associated with an office that worked that way. At least, to his credit, Steve still looked like the cop he had been rather than put on sartorial airs like this courtroom peacock. But the high-volume business did not leave time for real analysis of cases. It was churn- em and burn-em. After the client was signed by being told the case was really hard but the lawyer could win it, when they went to court the lawyers were always looking for a plea deal. When they got to court the client would hear that pleading guilty was the way to avoid a catastrophic time in prison.

This is what John was sure Oh Gee was leaning toward with Lady's case with the sex tossed in to make up for what he didn't get on their dates. John wasn't sure that the case against Gail was strong, but he was sure this guy was not really interested in finding out.

Oh Gee told Lady he had found out that Gail was charged along with another person with possession of a stolen check and an attempt to cash the check. He told her that she needed his expertise because there was a handwriting expert who was going to connect Gail to the check.

When John heard the facts of the arrest from the attorney, he wondered what was being left out. If the facts were what the attorney said he was told by a "friend" in the DA's office, John thought that any first-year public defender should be able to get the case against Gail thrown out.

Driving back to the lounge, John said, "Lady if this lawyer gave you the 10k to go to bed with him, at least you would only be getting fucked once. But if you paid him and had to have sex with him, then you'd be getting fucked twice."

Lady said she was willing to go with John's advice but not willing to go to court alone. She wanted him to go to court with her.

John hated watching other lawyers try cases. He even disliked watching lawyer programs on TV. Except for the show he watched with Carla, he often found himself yelling at the characters on the screen.

Very reluctantly, because he liked Lady, he told her he would go.

Later at the bar, Lady related to Carla the result of the office visit. She asked if Carla would come to court with them.

Carla realized the court date was set for the day after she had planned to leave, but she decided that she could pack all her belongings for the trip and leave from Ft. Lauderdale right after court.

TWENTY-ONE

In Los Angeles, Steve was pleased that his maneuvering had paid off. He called Marsha and was surprised when Mathew answered the phone. When she got on the phone Steve told her of that he managed to get a court date in two weeks in front of Red Davis.

He said that he would be in touch next week to tell her more about what to expect in court but in the meantime, he reminded her that should make sure she brought the copy of her marriage license and deed to the house. He was not sure she would need any of that but with his house closing on the new house coming up soon he didn't want to be in a situation where there was some last-minute delay.

He told her Dick Moran was going to be in court and he would testify about John's disappearance from the boat and with that—and the insurance company lawyer looking for a comfortable spot to lie down—hopefully they would have their money be the end of the month.

Now with the court date set, they finished talking about what to expect in court, Steve put Pam on the phone so she and Marsha could plan some sort of memorial service.

When Marsha hung up, she told Mathew what Steve had said. and the plans she was making with Pam.

He didn't say anything about the check, or of its arrival at the end of the month, but they both thought that after the court appearance and after the memorial they could start thinking about a church wedding.

Mathew, after moving in with her had put his house on the market and was delighted when his broker called to tell him that it looked like his status as a celebrity doctor had rubbed off on his house—she had two sets of buyers interested and they were each offering more than his asking price. She was happily going to push the bidding war as far as she could and try to set an early closing date.

TWENTY-TWO

After her decision not to hire Oh Gee, Lady visited Gail and told her what had happened. Lady was pleased that Gail took the situation in stride and understood it. Lady thought it showed some newfound maturity on Gail's part not to reproach her mother for a situation she herself created. She just hoped that what Lady had been told by John about the case against her looking very weak was true.

With the case in Ft. Lauderdale set for the end of the week, Carla told John. "I'm gonna go to court with my car fully packed and get on the road from there."

She smiled, "But I have a little problem."

"How can I help?"

"Well you know I was planning on leaving town on Thursday, right."

"Yeah."

"Well, I told the landlord that's when I was leaving and he rented the place. He wants his keys back on Thursday."

"OK. Good for him."

"Well, I was wondering. My car is going to be so full of my stuff that there is barely going to be room for me in the driver's seat. Do you think you could help me find a place to sleep Thursday night?"

John was already sad about the idea of her leaving. He knew that spending the night was not going to change her mind about that. He liked the idea of spending her last night with him even if he didn't like that it would be the last. Spending the whole night was something she had only done once before when they played the "room service" game. So, he played his part, he smiled, "Yes, dear."

The night before the court appearance John did not get much sleep. While Carla slept, he thought about the details of the last time he was in a courtroom. There in the dark, he smiled when he reminded himself of the good feeling he had about having gotten that case dismissed—"put to bed" as he liked to call it when he finished a case.

In Ft. Lauderdale, the case unfolded pretty much as John thought it would have to, according to what he had gleaned from listening to Lady and Oh Gee.

The first witness was a grocer who testified that he was in his store when a man he didn't know—but had seen around the neighborhood—came into his store to buy some groceries but said all he had was check for $150 for some work he had done for a man the grocer knew lived in the neighborhood.

The grocer told him he could not cash the check with the money he had on hand but he should be able to cash it near closing time around 5:30. The man with the check said he would come back then.

In the meantime, the man whose checkbook had been stolen came into the store lamenting that his home had been broken into his checkbook stolen. The grocer told him a man had come in to cash one of his checks and said he was coming back to the store later that afternoon. John noted that Gail's young lawyer raised no hearsay object to what the alleged victim said about his checkbook being stolen.

The grocer said that just before closing, two detectives came into the grocery, and the grocer told the police about the man returning and the police said they would to wait. As arranged, when the suspect came back, the grocer told him he still did not have the money.

Next, a detective testified that on the signal from the grocer, that this was the man who had come in before, the detective followed the suspect outside and arrested him as he was getting into a car with Gail whom he also arrested.

The last witness was a police department handwriting expert. He testified that he examined the check, and the handwriting sample the detectives had taken from Gail, and in his opinion the handwriting on the sample matched the handwriting that made out the face of the check.

Gail's lawyer cross-examined the expert about his training and methods and John squirmed in his seat as he watched and listened. Her attorney was asking questions in a way that allowed the expert to expand on his training and make him look more like an expert than he had before the cross-examination started. But the fact that he even bothered to cross-examine the witness led John to worry that Gail's lawyer had not seen the flaw in the case that John thought he should.

When her lawyer finished, he sat down. The prosecutor asked the court to have the evidence of the check and the handwriting sample admitted into evidence.

The judge looked at Gail's lawyer to see if there was any objection?

Her lawyer just sat there and then started to put his file in his overstuffed-with-cases briefcase.

John, realizing Gail's lawyer had no clue, found himself on his feet, "Objection your honor. No probable cause for the arrest. The handwriting exemplar is the fruit of the poisonous tree."

Everybody in the courtroom looked at John. He realized what had just happened, he grimaced, and sat back down.

The judge said, "Let's have no more outbursts from the cheap-seats." He thought about what John said, then nodded toward him, "Even if they are correct."

Looking down at Gail's lawyer who was still packing, the judge, trying to salvage the record, asked, "Isn't that what you were about to say Mr. Douglas?"

Douglas, looked up, "Er—"

Slam! The judge's gavel came down, "Good! Your objection is sustained. The Court finds that the defendant was only sitting in a car and there has been no other evidence presented which would lead the Court to conclude there was probable cause for her arrest. Therefore, since she was illegally in custody, the handwriting exemplar," and he again nodded to John, "is product of the illegal arrest and—as so colorfully referred to—is the fruit of the poisonous tree. It is inadmissible as evidence."

Looking down at Gail he said, "This case is dismissed. Your probation is reinstated back to when it was suspended. That being the case, your term of probation has expired. You will be transported back to the jail to retrieve your property, after that you are free to go."

Gail looked at Lady, sitting in the front row with John and Carla and cried, "Momma, I'd like to come home now."

Through tears, Lady mouthed, "I'd love that."

Carla hugged Lady. "I'm so happy for you. I'm so glad it worked out. I have to go now. Maybe our paths will cross again."

As Lady went over to arrange to pick up Gail outside the jail, Carla pushed past John. She turned and shook her head with displeasure.

She grimaced, "Congratulations. Nice win, you lying bastard."

John, still surprised by what he had done, was taken back by the comment.

She continued, "'Objection, Your Honor—' Huh, I've been in courts long enough to know a good lawyer when I see one. That courtroom etiquette is not what any crime reporter learns. 'Hand writing exemplar' and 'fruit of the poisonous tree' I feel stupid for not seeing it before. Now I know why you winced when that lawyer on TV drama walked into the well of court. Crime reporter? Bullshit! I guess I should have known. I've never seen any kind of reporter who didn't have stacks of notebooks.

"I don't like being lied to. I never lied to you about who I am, and I'm sorry you felt you had to lie to me and to everyone else. I don't know why you're not doing what you're so good at, but at this point I'm sure I don't have the time to care. I will tell you this—whatever the professor lost it was because it was taken from him. I only hope for your sake you don't wind up like him because you've thrown away all of who you really are."

John started to think of something smart to say but she turned and left.

As Lady came back, she saw Carla leave but had not heard what she said. She was just delighted that John had been right, although it looked like it was he, and not Gail's lawyer, who had gotten her free.

Wiping her tears she said, "You saved my little girl and you saved me too. I'm so happy she's coming home. You know you'll never have to pay for a drink at my place again, right?"

She smiled, "I'd even offer you what Oh Gee wanted from me, but I afraid Tione would be a tough act to follow."

It was late in the afternoon when John got home, he pulled into a parking spot in front of the stairs to his apartment, but he couldn't bring himself to get out of the car. He wasn't ready to face his empty apartment yet. He sat there and thought about what happened in court. He was pleased with the result. It felt good to know Lady was happy. He was pleased that he was right about the weakness of the case. But Carla's comparison to the professor hurt.

Not wanting to be sad, he started to tried to think of where he would go to celebrate a win if he were in LA. That only made him feel worse.

He decided to drive to Lady's lounge. It was a reluctant choice, almost a choice between non-choices. When he got there, he realized he wouldn't feel right there either. Carla's reproach, about lying to them all, stuck with him. He didn't fit there either.

As he drove out of the parking lot, he flipped on the radio and he headed for Miami Beach. He went over one of the causeways. Miami was beautiful. It was a clear night and all the lights reflected in the water.

He felt lost. A song started on the radio. He recognized the song, and turned the volume up. It was an old favorite. It was Harry Chapin's "W.O.L.D." It seemed like he was hearing some of the words for the first time.

He started to cry as the words sunk in— "Sometimes I get this crazy dream that I just take off in my car. But you can travel on ten thousand miles and still stay where you are."

John shook his head slowly from side to side. He thought, Crazy Dream. The vision of professor's hands and Carla's words flooded in on him. He remembered an epitaph that said that suicide was a miserable long solution to short-term problems. He thought, Still stay where you are and maybe still stay who you are. Maybe instead of jumping out of the boat I should have jumped out of my marriage and ended the partnership.

He headed back to his empty apartment. As he climbed the stairs, he reminded himself about how careful he had been in not creating any false identification. He had not broken any laws. He knew he could go back if he wanted to.

Up in his apartment, he went to the phone without even taking off his jacket.

It was done in less than a minute. He thought the call had the same impulsive driving force as his jump off the boat. The call took about the same amount of time as going into the water at the Marina.

He didn't mention Snappy or the money or even where he had been.

Making the call did not make him feel relieved. He was surprised—he thought it might.

After he put the phone down, he thought he should call back right away and go into more details but decided he couldn't. There would be time enough for that later. Maybe when he sorted out for himself what there was to tell in the first place.

He really didn't want to have to face any of it.

He just knew the call had to have been made. Maybe he'd want to go back to practice law the way he felt it should be. Maybe he could make it as a writer and he could use his real name to push forward with that. Or maybe he could do both.

Carla was right about lying. If he kept it up and he met someone he wanted to get serious with, who could he say he was? What was his story, his life's history?

No. He nodded to himself that the call was inevitable. He had had to do it. His trip was over. From now on, he was no longer running away. From now on, it was all going back.

But he would have to started thinking about what might have to be faced. Even though he had broken no laws, it was going to be a mountain of shit and he had no idea how he was going to deal with it.

Marsha was sitting on the corner of her bed pulling on her pantyhose getting dressed to go out to a Hollywood party with Mathew when the phone rang. She had to crawl across to the other side of the bed to get to the phone.

When she picked up the phone and listened, she knew right away it was long distance and in that split second before John spoke, she wondered who it could be.

The call was short. Thinking about it after, she realized she hadn't said a word other than "Hello."

John recognized her voice and called her by name rather than his old, "Hi sweets it's me."

This time it was, "Marsha. It's John. I know this is a bit of a shock. I am coming home. I have some things to work out with you and Steve. I will call you in a day or so when I get myself sorted out. If I didn't make this call right now, I might have lost the nerve but I don't think so—I have to come back home."

That was all he said. That was all he felt he could say. When he hung up the phone. He knew he had a long trip back to decide if he was going to use the excuse of being afraid of Snappy's killers or some sort of amnesia or not.

He would decide on the way home. But he was going home.

Marsha recognized his voice. She knew it was John.

She dropped the phone to the floor. Before she could pick it up and hang up, she lay face down on the bed. It took a while before she could move.

Mathew knew something was wrong.

He held her in his arms as she told him about the call. His thoughts raced as he called Steve but just said he needed to come over right away.

Steve said he'd be right over.

Mathew sat on the living room couch with Marsha. Steve paced the floor. The first question Steve asked, "Have you called Dick?

"No. I haven't called anyone."

"You're sure it was John."

She exhaled and nodded, "Yes. I'm sure."

"And he told you he would call back in a day or so?"

She nodded yes.

Steve's hands tightened into fists and relaxed.

He nodded to himself as he thought about Nick DelPesco. He was sure that Nick had enough juice to try tracing the call.

He looked down at the faces of Mathew to Marsha.

He took a deep breath as he studied them carefully

He stopped pacing and exhaled as he sat down across from them.

Steve saw that Mathew had his arm around Marsha and she was holding his other hand tightly.

Steve leaned forward on his couch so he could see their eyes and see what reaction they would have to what he was about to suggest.

"OK," he nodded slowly. "So, who else could know this son of a bitch is still alive?"

9 798986 725925